Robert Hogarth Patterson

Robespierre

A Lyrical Drama

Robert Hogarth Patterson

Robespierre
A Lyrical Drama

ISBN/EAN: 9783744787130

Printed in Europe, USA, Canada, Australia, Japan

Cover: Foto ©Andreas Hilbeck / pixelio.de

More available books at **www.hansebooks.com**

ROBESPIERRE

ROBESPIERRE

A LYRICAL DRAMA

BY

R. H. PATTERSON

AUTHOR OF

'ESSAYS IN HISTORY AND ART,' 'THE SCIENCE OF
FINANCE,' ETC.

*WITH A PREFACE ON THE NEW PHASE OF
THE MODERN DRAMA*

Printed for the Author
BY WILLIAM BLACKWOOD AND SONS
EDINBURGH AND LONDON
MDCCCLXXVII

DRAMATIS PERSONÆ.

CAMILLE, *a young Soldier of the Republic.*

ERNEST, *his Friend.*

ROBESPIERRE.

COLLOT, *a Republican of the Marat type.*

COUNT BEAUREGARD, *a Royalist Noble.*

RAYMOND, *Nephew of the Count.*

MARCEL, *an old Attendant of the Count.*

FRANÇOIS, *a Servant in the Count's household.*

LUCILLE, *Daughter of Count Beauregard.*

ANNETTE, *her Attendant.*

Nobles, Soldiers, Citizens, Choristers, &c.

PREFACE.

ON THE NEW PHASE OF THE MODERN DRAMA.

THE Drama is entering upon a new phase, in harmony with the altered conditions of Theatrical representation, and with the altered tastes of theatrical audiences. The scenery of the stage is more gorgeous, and also more faithful or realistic, than ever. What Charles Kean began, in his splendid Shakespearian revivals, has been continued, if not surpassed. And, along with this, an entirely new feature or phase of the Drama has recently been introduced ; and the success which has attended it shows that the change is, on the whole, an improvement. This new principle of dramatic construction may be described briefly as Simplicity of Scene. A Comedy has now only one Scene for each Act ; while Historical Plays, and the serious Drama generally, begin to exhibit a like restriction of scene, although to a lesser degree. This altered construction—which may be called an external or superficial change in the form of the drama—is also being accompanied by a different mode of dramatic treatment

a

which I believe will progress, and will involve a substan-
tial change in the character of the Drama itself. But
firstly, as to the external change—*i.e.*, in the form of
Construction.

This principle of construction is substantially different
from that hitherto adopted by our dramatists, from
Shakespeare down to Sheridan and Bulwer Lytton.
Shakespeare, the king of dramatic authors, in common
with most other dramatists in modern times, constructed
his dramas without any regard to Simplicity of Scene.
In most of his plays the scenes are exceedingly numerous,
and the changes of locality incessant. Taking three of
his leading dramas at random, we find that "Julius Cæsar"
has eighteen scenes, the "Merchant of Venice" nineteen,
and "Macbeth" twenty-eight, each of these twenty-eight
scenes being in a different locality. In Shakespeare's
Plays, as well as in those of subsequent English dramatists, each part of the plot is developed and acted on the
stage. The subordinate links of the story are clearly
represented. Even a dialogue which hardly fills a page
is assigned to its proper locality. The actual presentment of every incident or event was regarded as indispensable to the effective representation of the dramatic
story, however rapidly it might shift from one locality to
another. Thus the dullest imagination can easily and
vividly follow the thread of the story.

Shakespeare was a stage-manager as well as a great
dramatist, and therefore it cannot be said that he constructed his Plays in ignorance of stage requirements;
and there is every reason to believe that his Plays were

acted as he wrote them.   It is not less true that in recent times the minor scenes have been omitted on the stage, and the changes of locality (though still numerous) are diminished.   And now, within the last few years, Simplicity of Scene has become one of the first things sought for in a new drama.   How was it, then, that a great dramatic artist like Shakespeare, possessing not only peerless creative genius, but also a perfect knowledge of dramatic representation, so freely introduced changes of locality, obviously paying no regard to restriction of scene?   Or rather, perhaps, we should ask, Why does the newest form of the Modern Drama adopt the opposite course?   I think it will be found—as might well be expected—that Shakespeare's practice was quite right, indeed superior to any other, for his own time, as indeed for many generations afterwards ; and that the preference now given to Simplicity of Scene is owing to a great change which has recently occurred in the conditions of dramatic representation.

I believe the almost universal answer to the question above asked would be, that the very splendour of the scenery nowadays necessitates a restriction in the number of the scenes, owing to their costliness.   Working upon Shakespeare's masterpieces, Charles Kean successfully disregarded the element of first-cost ; but few managers would do this for a new play ; and under any circumstances, multiplicity of scenery is objectionable on the ground of expense.   In old times, this element of cost did not exist.   In Shakespeare's time, and until a quite recent date, the scenery of the stage was of the slightest description. Sometimes the change of scene or locality was indicated merely by hanging up a placard, announcing that "This is Venice "—"This is the Wood of Ardennes"—"This is Rome"—"This is Macduff's Castle," or the like. Certainly little or no attempt was made to represent the locality faithfully or realistically. In one old play, where two of the characters meet and quarrel in a town, and adjourn to the suburbs to fight a duel, they merely take a few steps across the stage, and then stop and say, "Now we are at the town's end," and proceed to business. In such times, when no regard was paid to the actual representation of localities, it is obvious that little or no objection would arise as to frequent changes of the scene on the ground of expense ; whereas nowadays the cost of putting plays on the stage is sometimes very great.

I fully admit that this question of expense has much to do with the new mode of dramatic construction on the principle of Simplicity of Scene. Nevertheless, I believe that this is far from being an adequate explanation of the change, much less a justification of it. I believe that the cause of the change is both wider and higher than a question of cost. It is the approval and support of the Public that makes a play pecuniarily successful, — not merely the comparative economy with which it is put on the stage ; and if Simplicity of Scene did not find favour with the Public, the new dramas constructed on this principle would not be so favoured by theatrical managers as they are. Let the subject be thoughtfully considered, and I think that the new form of dramatic construction will be found to be justified by true principles of Art, which, at least in their practical effect, are appreciated and approved by our theatrical audiences.

Simplicity of Scene is really a revival of the old doctrine of the dramatic "Unities" of Time and Place. The "Unities" have long been scouted in this country as utterly false and antiquated canons of dramatic art ; and undoubtedly, as usually preached, the doctrine was a mistake, inasmuch as it was made applicable to the Drama universally, and irrespective of certain circumstances or conditions of the stage, without which the observance of the unities would be not only unrequired, but disadvantageous. The doctrine of the unities was educed from a study of the Greek Tragedies, the dramatic masterpieces of the old world, and peerless still of their kind ; but the authors and supporters of the doctrine erred in this, that they overlooked the peculiarities which belonged to the old Greek Drama, and imagined that the law of the unities, so imperative, natural, and successful on the Athenian stage, sought to be likewise imperative, and equally natural, in the Theatre as it existed in the time of Shakespeare and in the Drama of modern Europe generally.

The Athenian Drama was wholly unlike the Drama of Shakespeare or of modern Europe. It stands alone, as a peculiar type, hitherto without a parallel. It had more points of resemblance with the Opera, the Oratorio, and the great and solemn periodical performances of the Passion-Play at Ammergau—much nearer still to a combination of these forms of dramatic and musical art.

Like the Oratorio and the Passion-Play, the Greek Drama
dealt with themes and events well known in their outlines
to the audience—the national legends, always solemn, if
not also tragic, which were to the Greeks very much what
Bible subjects are to Christendom. There were no " surprises," and little dramatic action. It was a stately tale
splendidly put on the stage ; and the special charm and
attraction were the poetic grandeur and beauty of the
dialogue, developing solemn event and high-wrought emotion, heightened by intermingled music and the songs of
the Chorus, together with the choral dances, expressive of
passion and sentiment—in most of these respects resem-
bling the modern Opera, where the special charm is not
that of dramatic event, but a splendid development of the
Emotions connected with the events. A well-known
legend was depicted at its culminating point, and the
antecedent and accessory events were described in the
dialogue or by the chorus—the songs of the chorus, too,
serving to cover any slight transitions in time. From all
those circumstances a single scene or tableau sufficed for
the whole Drama. Thus the unities of Time and Place
were maintained, owing to the essential conditions of the
Drama ; while the third unity, that of Sentiment (as to
which the greatest mistake of all was made by modern
critics), arose naturally, if not of necessity, from the
themes chosen for representation, which were uniformly
solemn, like those of the modern Oratorio and Passion-
Plays ; while the music and choral appliances prevented
the sensation of monotony which otherwise would have
accompanied the unities of Scene and Sentiment.

The Greek Play, however, lacked one potent charm of the modern stage. The *rôle* of the Actor was, of necessity, restricted by the vastness of the Greek Theatre—which in some cases was fitted to contain 20,000 people. In so vast a place, the effect of facial expression, the play of feature, would have been wholly lost, and was not attempted—the *rôle* of the actor being restricted to splendid elocution, accompanied by graceful and impressive, but somewhat statuesque, attitude. Let this single fact be mentally realised, and the wide difference between the Greek Play and the modern stage will become strikingly apparent. What would the finest drama on the modern stage become if the *rôle* of the actor were similarly restricted? It is obvious that in proportion as the attractive powers of the actor are restricted, the greater is the demand made upon the dramatic skill and poetic genius of the Author, and also upon the resources and attractive appliances of the Theatre: and the Poets and the Theatre of Athens were equal to the trying task imposed upon them. Finally, let it be said—if it need to be said—that the Greek Plays were performed before a cultured and highly critical audience, consisting solely of the educated "citizens," men of property and culture,—the lower classes, or large body of domestics and operatives, who in Athens constituted about four-fifths of the population (who were " slaves," but not in the harsh sense attached to the word in modern times), being wholly excluded.

Art-rules of every kind are simply deductions made by critics from a thoughtful contemplation of the masterpieces of Art; and when the Drama was revived in

Europe, the Greek Tragedies were the model naturally adopted by the art-critics who laid down the canons for dramatic composition. The fact, however, was overlooked that the canons of composition in the Greek Drama were absolute only in regard to that peculiar type of drama. Moreover, the unities of Time and Place were rather valuable accessaries than fundamental canons of that grand style of dramatic composition; or at least, the observance of these unities arose so naturally from, and combined so readily with, the general structure and fundamental art-object of the Greek Drama, that any violation of them was unnecessary, and therefore the loss of " realism " from their violation would have been peculiarly objectionable.

The "classic" drama of France and Italy, which dealt solely with serious and heroic themes, was professedly based upon the old Greek Tragedies, but the resemblance was of the most meagre description. The dramas of Corneille, Racine, and Voltaire do not really correspond at all with the Greek Plays; and indeed, as I shall by-and-by show, a revival of the grand Geek type of drama in those times was practically impossible. This pseudo-classic drama aimed at copying the Greek drama in its observance of the unities, especially the unity of sentiment; a brilliant heroism and the love-passion taking the place of that uniformity of gloom which (so strangely for so lively a people) pervaded the drama of the Greeks. But the music, the chanting, the lyric poetry, and all the rich choral appliances, which were of the very essence of the Athenian drama, and which acted like pleasing variations on the dominant theme, were wholly wanting. Nor could the unities of time and place be observed in a manner corresponding to the Greek Drama, owing to the exigencies of the story, which was always unfamiliar to the audiences, and frequently of the author's own invention. Even the verse-dialogue, grand, polished, and sonorous as it was, was monotonous, and lacked the richer and more varied melody of the Greek. Finally, in the time of these modern-classic dramatists, the Scenery of the theatre was so defective that the prime motive for observing the unities of time and place hardly existed.

With this passing remark on the pseudo-classic dramas of France and Italy, I shall now restrict what I have to say to our own Drama, the drama of Shakespeare, which the German Drama has largely followed, and which, since Classicism went out of vogue at the end of last century, may almost be said to represent the serious Modern Drama generally.

Shakespeare, by far the greatest genius in the Modern Drama, or indeed of all time, wholly disregarded the unities; and there were good reasons for his doing so. In the first place, in common with the other dramatists of Europe, Shakespeare worked upon a class of subjects which differed considerably in character from those of the Athenian Drama, especially relative to the audience: Biblical subjects, indeed, being in his time almost the only ones akin to the themes of the Greek Drama, alike in the solemnity of their character and in their familiarity to the audience; and even in his historical plays he does not rely upon his audience's familiarity with the story. Shakespeare and the modern dramatists have relied greatly in their plays upon the interest of Event, dramatic surprises—in short, the novelty of the story presented to the audiences: whereas, as already said, this element of interest had hardly any place in the Greek Drama, where the subject was some familiar legend, and where the great attraction was the representation of the story at its culminating single phase, giving the grandest portrayal of the emotions connected with it which poetry, music, and expressive or pantomimic dance could accomplish. The Modern Drama has prized Novelty of event and dramatic surprises so much, that its highest aim and achievement has been to invent the tales which it depicts; and hence a multiplicity of scenes has hitherto been found indispensable in order to make the plot intelligible and the drama effective. Moreover, the theatrical audiences of modern Europe have desired to see all the events *acted*. Partly from their inferior culture, partly from the absence of the rich emotional accessaries of the Greek stage, *seeing* was necessary for their believing, or at least for the adequate stirring of their emotions.

The third unity—viz., of Sentiment, was thoroughly discarded by Shakespeare: it was not merely neglected (so to speak) like the two other unities, but he deliberately and systematically violated it as incompatible with the variety of incident and emotion upon which he so much relies. It was not merely that Shakespeare saw that human nature is very composite, and that in life the mean and the noble, the humorous and the sad, keep close company. It is evident that he blended humour, even buffoonery, with the grave or tragic, often in the closest conjunction, not merely because these frequently coexist in real life, but also as an artistic appliance, whereby the interspersed levity serves to heighten by contrast the effect of the pathetic or terrible, as well as gives a relief, momentary but valuable, to the high-wrought sensations produced by tragedy. Witness for example the grave-diggers in "Hamlet," the drunken porter's soliloquy in "Macbeth," interjected between the murder of the king and its discovery, and dozens of other instances.

Thus the difference between the Athenian and the Shakespearian Drama—the "Classic" and the "Romantic" —as regards the unities, arises in part from the different class of subjects which they deal with, and still more from the difference of the elements of interest upon which they respectively rely. I think it will be acknowledged, however, that the difference has been also due to another cause, hitherto little remarked, and not so agreeable to modern vanity—namely, to a real and great inferiority of the Modern Theatre to the Greek, and hence also of our Drama regarded as a theatrical representation, a work of art depicted or developed on the stage.

When the Drama was revived in Europe, it was absolutely impossible (even if the desire had existed) to adopt the model of the Greek Plays. A great gulf lay between the Classic world and the Renaissant world of modern Europe. The grand and highly-developed civilisation of Greece and Rome had perished under a landslip of Northern barbarism ; and the Drama revived while the now dominant Races of Europe were merely struggling out of conditions of life which would have been utter barbarism to the Athenian Greeks or the Imperial Roman. In Art as in Politics, and in the general amenities of life and society, Europe had to begin anew. The Theatre, in which the Greeks had excelled, and which both with them and the Romans was a great popular entertainment, shared the same fate. It was almost devoid of scenery and costume, and wholly lacking in professional choristers and musicians or in the skilfully trained symbolic or pantomimic dancers of the Classic world. It is true that, so early as Shakespeare's time, the arts of painting and music had been successfully revived, but they existed apart from the Theatre,—they formed no part of its appliances; and though in later times these arts might be evoked in Court Masks and pageantries, down even to recent times they had no regular place in the Theatre as a popular entertainment— which in Classic times was, and ever must be, the especial character of the Drama, the most democratic of all the Fine Arts.

The Poetry was there, and in the hands of Shakespeare, and some other great dramatists, it reached an excellence quite equal of its kind, though not usually in its variety, to that of the masterpieces of Greece; but that was all. To have placed a Greek Drama on the stage in those times (as has been done recently), or any play constructed on the Greek model, would have been altogether vain : it could have attained no higher attraction than that of fine elocution of fine poetry—a bald and meagre performance, which indeed might almost as well have been spoken by a single actor, because the realism even of costume was wanting. Hence, I repeat, it was impossible to follow the Greek models of dramatic construction, even if Shakespeare and his compeers had been familiar with them. And hence, if the Drama, as revived, was to be what is its essence, a *popular* entertainment, some other and potent elements of interest must be introduced in order to compensate the loss of the special attractions of the Theatre as a spectacular and artistic performance. There had been Passion-Plays of the rudest kind, as *quasi* religious performances; but if the Drama was to assume a high as well as popular form, some new elements must be introduced. As it was impossible to present grand and splendid legendary or historical tableaux like those of the Greek Drama, with all the attractions of fine scenery and costume, accompanied by music and the dance, the bare walls of the modern stage were made attractive by novelty of story, and also by the triumphs of the Actor, who has obtained a far wider sphere for dramatic representation than was afforded him on the Athenian stage. And novelty of story necessarily brought with it many changes of Time and Place (although, be it noted, not at first to any great extent of Scenery): thus disregarding the "Unities," and launching the Modern Drama upon a widely different course from that of the classic drama of Greece.

A different and simpler form of the Drama arose. In proportion as the Spectacle was weak, and music absent, the greater must be the appeal to the unaided mind. The

lack or baldness of scenery and other artistic adjuncts
not only allowed (by minimising the effect upon the
spectators of changes of locality), but actually fostered,
if not rendered imperative, the Novelty of incident which
have characterised the Modern Drama. The masterpieces
of the Modern Drama are original creations — acted
Novels, so to speak—like "Othello," "Hamlet," "The
Tempest," and many other plays of Shakespeare, and
in recent times like the "Hunchback," the "Lady of
Lyons," and other poetic dramas, not to speak of the
prose drama, which can boast of pieces of high theatrical
attractions.

Thus, although the Modern Drama has possessed works
of the highest genius and poetry—Shakespeare, Calderon,
Corneille and Racine, Goethe and Schiller, forming a
galaxy of dramatists fully equal (to say the least) to those
of Greece and Rome, and far more varied in their themes
—the *Theatre* has been in its infancy—deficient in all the
requirements of the stage, save Poetry and the genius of
the Actor. It is only now, within the present generation,
that the Theatre has been enriched by those artistic and
realistic accessaries which properly belong to it, and which
existed in perfection in the palmy days of Greece. Accordingly, it is only now that dramas similar, or approaching in kind and construction, to those of Sophocles and his
illustrious compeers, could possibly be produced and rendered effective as popular entertainments. And exactly
in proportion as the Modern Theatre is reaching perfection, do we not begin to perceive better than before how
much there is to be said in favour of the ancient Greek

type of drama? Nay more, are not the requirements of the perfected Theatre *tending* towards a revival of such-like pieces? And are not dramatists beginning to compose more in accordance with these requirements, so far at least as regards the unities? In this respect, indeed, are not one or two of the newest high-class dramas constructed (whether consciously or not by the author does not matter) to a remarkable extent upon the model of the classic drama of Greece?

We may be sure that the highly-cultured Greeks—the dramatists and audiences of Athens, "the eye of Greece" —had a good reason, and for themselves at least a sufficient one, for the peculiar form which their Drama assumed in its culminating period. It has been said that the Greeks were like artists who destroyed their first sketches—the Greek Drama (and, in the main, Greek Art of all kinds) appearing to us of later times as if it had sprung into existence perfect and peerless—only its masterpieces having been preserved. But undoubtedly the Greek Theatre had an infancy as bald and meagre as that of Modern Europe—without scenery or costume, and with music and dance only of the rudest kind—in fact, merely an acted or recited dialogue. Why, then, did it eschew novelty of story? and why did it eschew the frequent changes of scene and redundant display of action which characterise the Modern Drama — preferring to depict the story in what may be called a grand tableau, whereby the Unities of Time and Place were faithfully observed? I think it probable, indeed certain, that but for the downfall of Greek Art, novelty of story would ere long have been adopted by the Greek dramatists. Fiction or imaginative literature, whether in prose or verse, comes late, and is rarely had recourse to so long as Legend or History supply adequate themes for the muse. But I do not think that the Greek Drama would ever have much departed from its peculiar model as regards construction. Not only were the Greeks a symmetry-loving people (while we of the Gothic or northern races prefer variety), but I think that the Greek Drama, as an artistic and essentially theatrical performance, and appealing to a cultured audience, was superior to any other form which the Drama has since assumed. I have said that the observance of the unities was by no means the prime object of the peculiar structure of the Greek Drama, but it was a valuable adjuvant to the *illusion of reality*, and thereby heightened the effect of the grand portrayal of the Passions or Emotions which *was* the prime object of the high drama of Athens. The grand works of Æschylus, Sophocles, and Euripides were composed *for the Theatre*—to be represented on the stage, with all its perfected appliances of scenery and costume, music and the ballet, and to a highly critical and intelligent audience. And, viewed in this light, I cannot conceive any form of the drama equal to that of ancient Greece, especially if performed in a smaller theatre where the triumphs of the actor could be fully enjoyed.

I think we may accept it as a truth, that even the Court of Xerxes, far off as it was, was more faithfully, as well as more splendidly, represented in the " Persæ " on the stage of Athens 2500 years ago, than (*e.g.*) the

Court of Venice was in "Othello" on the British stage
at the beginning of the present century. Exactly
in proportion as the Scenery is perfect, the changes
of scenery become objectionable ; they impair the illusion of Realism, which is the highest attainment of the
Theatre, *quâ* Theatre. The Theatre is pre-eminently a
spectacle,—θεατρον, a thing to be seen ; and the Greek
Dramas were magnificent poetry, giving voice to the
events, but far more to the Emotions of the story, exclud-
ing all incidents whose representation on the stage would
be glaringly unreal, and without any change of place or
noticeable change of time, thereby maintaining the illusion
of reality to the fullest possible extent ; while the emotion
was further heightened, the general effect enriched, and
the æsthetic tastes of the audiences gratified and fully
satisfied by music and the choral dance.

Besides the respect for the unities, as a means of maintaining the precious illusion of reality, there was undoubtedly another cause for the peculiar structure adopted
in the perfected Greek Drama. In their Art-tempera-
ment the Greeks, and especially the Athenians, differed
greatly from the Romans, who in their robust hard-mind-
edness and comparative sluggishness of mental sensibility,
approached more nearly to the peoples of Renaissant
Europe. The Greeks were admittedly a highly suscep-
tible and impressionable people — a narrative-picture
recited to them in splendid verse impressed them almost
as much as the actual presentment of the scene would do
an ordinary modern audience. The representation of a
murder or violent death on the stage would have shocked

b

them most disagreeably, as indeed it begins to do audiences nowadays : and the narration of such events, which abounded in their tragedies, produced as vivid an impression through the imagination as was requisite or artistically agreeable. This liveliness of imagination, this quick response of emotion to mere words without action, or rather to the vivid descriptions of recited poetry, was indispensable to the success of the Greek form of drama, wherein not merely tragic and painful events were excluded from the stage, but almost the whole *action* of the Play,—the genius of the dramatist, as I have already said, being mainly devoted, not to the representation of the events, but of the emotions connected with the events— which, I venture to say, is likewise the grand *motive* of the modern Opera. The common opinion that it was the painfulness of the leading events which caused their non-representation in the Greek drama is only half true ; for I repeat, nearly the whole of the action was excluded from the stage. For example, in " Hecuba," not only the murder of Polydore, the sacrifice of Polyxena, and the mutilation of the Thracian king, and the murder of his sons by the Trojan dames, but also the finding of the body of Polydore on the shore, the apparition of the shade of Achilles gleaming in his golden armour above his tomb, —all these incidents are excluded alike from actual representation. And why ? Partly because it was impossible to represent them while maintaining the illusion of reality ; and also because, owing to the liveliness of the Greek imagination, their representation was not necessary to the realisation of those incidents, when narrated in splendid verse; while, I must repeat, the grand motive of the Greek drama was the portrayal of the Emotions (rather than of the events) in the highest form which Poetry, spectacle, music, and the choral dance could achieve.

In corroboration of the opinion which I have just expressed (and which will hardly be questioned), that the Greeks, with their cultivated taste and their perfected Theatre, *deliberately* gave their æsthetic judgment in favour of their peculiar form of Drama, or of dramatic construction, I may refer to the Trilogies of Æschylus and Sophocles, and doubtless of other Athenian dramatists. _ In these Plays a whole story or career was represented; but each part of the Trilogy was constructed like a single Play, with complete observance of the dramatic unities. The story was told in three distinct Tableaux, in which each stage of the story was depicted at its culminating point, wherein all the incidents of that section of the story were skilfully gathered to a focus, partly depicted and partly related in one scene, upon the same spot or locality, so that there was no disturbance of the illusion of Realism. Thus, while in a great measure anticipating the comprehensiveness of the Modern Drama, the Greeks still adhered systematically to the unities and other elements essential to the illusion of Realism; whereas the Modern Drama in its long and brilliant career has paid little or no regard at all to the dramatic unities, or indeed to the possibilities of theatrical representation—lively dramatic *action* being necessary to atone for the baldness of the performance in other respects; and even now, when the Theatre has recovered its old perfection, changes of scene are considered objectionable merely or mainly owing to the expense which they entail upon the management.

But Modern Europe is not Classic Greece; and we may expect a characteristic difference between the Drama of Gothic Europe and that of Athens. The difference of Race will assert itself on the Stage as in other departments of Art, or indeed more so, owing to the essentially popular or democratic character of the Theatre. Just as in Architecture, the Northern races developed a style of their own, which reached its perfection in the magnificent Gothic cathedral—a style in which the dead stone is made to assume the forms of life and growth, rising aloft in the pillars like the clustered stems and over-roofing arcades of the forest, or budding into flowery knots at the corbeilles, or soaring like lambent flame in the window-traceries— a style full of life and variety, and in which even the grand solemnity of the whole is interspersed with details in which the artists made room for the grotesque: a grander and wider perfection than that even of Greek Art, and wholly different in character from the pure lovely symmetry and sunnyness of the classic style.

It is impossible to lay down any absolute rules for the Drama, or for any of the Fine Arts; indeed, next to Poetry, the Drama admits of greater variety of structure and treatment than any of the sister Arts; and the fact that it is the most popular or democratic of all the Arts, augments the sphere of its varieties according to the varying tastes and culture of the audiences. Therefore, there may be successful dramas of very various kinds; but it is chiefly of the poetic or tragic drama that I now write. As seems to me, what peculiarly belongs to the Drama of Modern Europe, and also which will last under all conditions of the Stage, is the element of Romance and Variety, of incident and emotion. The grandest works of the Drama will continue to be those in which creative imagination predominates: in which, together with perfection of language and faithful portrayal of character, the interest of the audience is excited by novelty of story or event, and generally, with a variety and contrast of emotion such as held no place in the masterpieces of the classic drama, wherein (whether solely from the symmetry-loving taste of the Greeks, or partly from the nature of the subjects considered suitable for their serious Drama) the unity of Sentiment was observed, if possible, even more stringently than those of Time and Place. And in this prevailing form of the Modern Drama an observance of the unities is almost impossible: there must be changes of time and of locality corresponding with the stages of the plot or story.

But is this modern style or structure of the Drama compatible with a perfection of theatrical representation? Is it such that would have arisen under, or can it appropriately co-exist with, a perfect and fully developed theatre? Or, at least, is not some modification of it called for æsthetically by the now-attained perfection and Realism of stage scenery, and also by the fuller and richer Art-accessaries? The Modern Drama seeks to combine novelty of story and dramatic surprises with realistic scenic representation : but can these elements of interest be perfectly combined ? The Modern Drama includes a far wider field of incident and event than the old Greek Drama, and also excites a much livelier interest in ordinary audiences ; but does it really admit of an equal degree of Theatrical excellence ? Upon this point we cannot appeal to the great example of Shakespeare—nor indeed to the practice of the illustrious host of Dramatists, either of this or other countries, down to Bulwer Lytton and the present generation : for it is only during the present generation, and almost within the last few years, that the Scenery of the Stage has become alike splendid and faithful or realistic—regaining the scenic perfection which was possessed in the palmy days of Athens. The question is rather, Would Shakespeare have constructed his Plays as he did had the Theatre been equal to what it has become now ? In fact, has not the *construction* of the Modern Drama, with its prevailing disregard of the unities of Time and Place, been owing partly, and in a very great degree, to the fact that the Theatre was then in its infancy, where " realism " of scenic effect was impossible—nay, where Scenery, until lately, was hardly thought of, or worthy of the name—and where the effects of the Theatre were confined to the interest of the tale, the poetry or beauty of language, and the attractive graces and impressiveness of the accomplished Actor ? And has not the increased culture of the audience produced new requirements ? Is it not the fact that the Shakespearian dramas have to be greatly altered in representation, now that the Theatre is being perfected, limiting the action and condensing the scenes — although Shakespeare composed his dramas expressly for the stage of his day, meaning every one of the scenes to be acted; and would not Shakespeare have approved of these modern alterations, or at least have constructed his dramas more in accord with the principle of these alterations, had the Theatre in his time been as perfect, *quâ* Theatre, as it is now?

Each of the Fine Arts has a special range or function; each of them has to submit to limitations or to adopt compromises; and these limitations and compromises are different for each Art, according to the materials or appliances with which it works, and to the organs of Sense to which it specially appeals or addresses itself. In Sculpture, Form; in Painting, Colour and Form, but specially Colour; in Music, Melody and the expression of Emotion; in Poetry, which has the widest range of all the Arts, the charm may consist in Narrative, in Thought or Idea, and in Emotion of all kinds, but only sparingly in physical description, or in all of these combined. Poetry appeals to the Mind alone, to the intellectual perceptions, without producing any impression upon the physical organs like the Eye and the Ear. Poetry presents only *words*, and the sensations, whether of Object or Emotion (powerful though these, and especially the latter, often are), are produced at second-hand, as it were, as a conseqence of the purely Mental perceptions only,—instead of also from a direct presentation to the physical organs of the Objects themselves, as in Sculpture and Painting to the Eye, or of the material causes of Emotion as in the sounds of Music. Thus in Painting, Sculpture, and Music, the impression is

made upon the physical organs, and also upon the Mind,
—upon the Eye or Ear *plus* Mind ; whereas Poetry is perceived by and makes its impression upon the Mind alone,
without conveying its impressions through or making any
impression upon the physical organs,—the rich and manifold sensations of Object or Emotion which it ultimately
produces being occasioned by the reflex action of the
Mind or Imagination upon the other Senses, and not from
any direct action upon the bodily senses themselves.

Thus, in *reading* a Drama, the Mind, the intellectual
perceptions, are the supreme, and in the first instance the
sole, judge,—the Emotions, and also the impressions of
external objects, being awakened and excited after the
cause of them has been perceived and appreciated by the
Mind. On the Stage, however, it is the Eye, together
with the Ear, that is specially addressed, and upon which
the primary impressions are made ; and what strikes the
Eye, and through it the Mind, has of necessity a stronger
influence than that which addresses the Mind or reflecting
organ alone ; because the physical organs convey impressions more instantly and forcibly to the Self than the less
vivid and slower-moving organs of reflection or intellectual
perception.

Hence, on the Stage, if there be a conflict as to Realism between the Eye and the Mind, the compromise ought,
as far as possible, to go in favour of the Eye. In reading
a Drama, the very reverse is true. Accordingly a sacrifice
to Simplicity of Scene which may be advantageous on
the Stage may prove very objectionable in the drama as
printed and read—*i.e.*, as addressing itself purely to the

Mind. But as every Drama worthy of the name—not simply a poem in Dialogue—is meant for the Theatre, it is the requirements of the Theatre which must be primarily attended to. I can well conceive of cases, however, in which the printed Drama should, for the adequate depictment of the Story to the mind, observe some changes of scene which on the Stage may be dispensed with, for the fuller maintenance to the Eye of the illusion of Reality.

In former times when the Theatre hardly ever sought to represent the locality, much less realistically, changes of scene—or rather changes of Time and Place, without any change of scenery—were equally little thought of by the Author or felt by the audience. The mind of the audience made a note of it—which, so far, was advantageous, indeed indispensable—but that was all : there was no shock to the illusion, because little or no change was presented to the eye,—the changes of *Scene*, in fact, may almost be said to have taken place without any visible change of locality. Thus, whatever Shakespeare may have thought, as an abstract question (if he thought of it at all), as to the unities of Time and Place, the effect upon the audience of his violations of those unities was of little account as a shock to Realism—the illusion of the Stage being then of the slightest description ; while his method of dramatic construction was undoubtedly superior to any other as a popular and readily intelligible depictment of the Story to the mind of the audience, and also to the reader of his Plays. Indeed I must repeat that Shakespeare's method, which has been that of our Modern Drama generally, was not only comparatively

unobjectionable owing to the baldness or total lack of
realistic scenery, but was in a great degree indispensable
owing to the novelty of the tales or stories which he set
before his audience, besides giving the fullest play to the
powers of the actor.   And I may add that the " conden-
sation of scene," if I may so describe it, which is now more
or less applied to his dramas, is rendered practicable and
advantageous greatly owing to the circumstance that the
subjects of his Plays—Shakespeare's Tales—have nowadays become " familiar as household words," and are as
well known to British audiences as were the legends of
Greece to the cultured audiences of Athens.

Nowadays the Scenery of the Stage is not only splendid,
but eminently faithful or realistic ; and on both of these
accounts, changes of scene, the transition from one locality
to another, produce a correspondingly greater impression
upon the audience : this in fact is the very object, or at
least the necessary consequence, of the Realism of the
Scenery.   The eye of the spectator sees one distinct and
realistically-portrayed locality pass away suddenly, and
another equally distinct and realistically-portrayed locality
take its place : and every such change is more or less a
drawback upon the realism of the mimic world upon which
the spectators are gazing.   Hence, frequent changes of
scenery are far more disillusionising than formerly, and
accordingly they ought to be adopted more sparingly, and
with more precautions, than they used to be when the
Theatre was still in its infancy.

It now becomes apparent, I think, that the doctrine of
" the Unities," fully practised in ancient Greece, contains

far more artistic truth and dramatic wisdom than have generally been attributed to it. And are we not coming back to it—not as a reaction, but as a progression—in exact proportion as the modern Theatre is becoming perfected, regaining the splendour and full appliances of the Athenian Stage, while, as a co-relative change, our audiences are becoming more cultured? *Simplicity of Scene* —which in its essence is the observance of the unities of Time and Place, and likewise involves the exclusion of much of the impossible action which abounds in our old plays—is becoming imposed upon the Drama as a resultant effect of the improvement of the Stage—of the great advance recently made in Theatrical representation as regards splendour and realism of scenery. I shall show, from some of the most recent dramas, that this change is being actually accomplished to a very remarkable extent, —and not by the scissors, or any mere *tour de force* of the Management, but by deliberate purpose and action of the Authors themselves. Of itself, this is a move in the right direction ; but first, let me say a word as to the necessary limitations upon Simplicity of Scene, lest a good precept be carried too far, and also as to the fuller development of the artistic appliances of the Theatre, which ought, more or less, to accompany this reversion towards the observance of the " dramatic unities."

In the first place, Simplicity of Scene—or the Unity of Time and Place—is apt to create an improbability, a disillusionment (if I may use so cumbrous a word), in place of the one which it supplants. In such a case, impossibility of Scene, which means unnaturalness of Event, takes the place of the shock produced by a visible yet impossible change of locality. The Mind is shocked instead of the Eye; or rather, while the visual sense is satisfied, the reflecting sense is outraged. In Farce this does not matter—indeed, the grotesqueness or broad caricature which forms the primary object of a Farce may even be heightened by the incongruity of persons making their appearance under the most improbable circumstances; while in Burlesque, now so popular a form of theatrical entertainment, the audience only laugh the more when Bluebeard, or the wicked Magician in "Aladdin," or other hero of the piece, after being stabbed through and through by many swords, either boldly disregards the fact, merely exclaiming, "Don't tickle me!" or else, after falling dead, gets up and joins in the grand break-down dance or song which closes the performance. In Comedy, also, at least of the lighter sort, the characters may, and do, come and go upon the scene under very improbable circumstances, without the mind of the amused and laughing audience taking note of the incongruity. In the Serious Drama, especially of the Shakespearian kind, however, the limitations upon Simplicity of Scene become more or less indispensable and imperative. Were our dramatists to revert to the actual Greek type, then the unities might be fully maintained with little difficulty; but, though some plays of this kind may be successfully composed, no general reversion to the pure Greek type is either to be expected or desired. Whether we take the Plays of Shakespeare, the high-class Comedies of Goldsmith and Sheridan, or the brilliant Dramas of Bulwer Lytton, it is wholly impossible to represent them on the Stage without comparatively frequent changes of locality, and corresponding changes of the scenery, appropriate to the successive stages of the story. This kind of drama will ever maintain its high place. Nevertheless the art of the Dramatist will be taxed to a degree unknown, because hitherto unrequired, to concentrate the action and minimise the changes of locality. And in carrying out this object some compromise must at times be made ; and I repeat that the observance of the dramatic unities in this manner may be successfully carried out on the Stage, to the Eye, to a degree which would be objectionable, and resented as an outrage by the Mind, in a drama as printed for the reading public.

Two other limitations or considerations have to be stated on this subject. Although the unities of Time and Place, which are involved in Simplicity of Scene, are valuable aids to the illusion of Reality on the Stage, variety of scene is also, *per se*, advantageous as adding to the richness of spectacular effect. In the Theatre, the Eye ought to be pleased and charmed to the fullest extent compatible with the other requirements of the Drama. Scenery even of the finest kind palls if kept long before the audience. The Greek Plays, where only one Scene was represented, were much shorter than the corresponding Five-Act serious dramas of Modern Europe ; and those single-scene dramas were enriched by attractive accessaries, or indeed essentials, which hitherto have been almost absent from our Serious Drama—namely, by elaborate music and the choral dance. It is only by fully regarding this *ensemble* of attractions or artistic appliances that we shall adequately appreciate the classic drama of Athens, which remains peerless of its kind, and towards which there is now a visible return in some of the most successful of our recent Plays.

In domestic and fanciful comedy, Robertson, Albury, and Gilbert have made us familiar with three-act pieces, with a single scene to each act—which is the Greek Trilogy applied to the lighter forms of the Drama. But the really difficult task was to revive this form of con-struction in the serious or heroic Drama. And this has been done to a considerable, or indeed remarkable, ex-tent and with great success by Mr Wills. His " Charles I.," the most successful of his plays, is a close approach to the Greek Trilogy, depicting the life of the " royal martyr " in separate scenes or tableaux, in which are skilfully concentrated and represented the leading incidents and circumstances of each stage of his career. The opening scene at Hampton Court depicts the amiable but ill-fated monarch at home, ending with the first mutterings of the gathering storm ; the second scene, at Whitehall, depicts the monarch and his opponents in the thick of the political strife ; and the third scene represents him in the War, at its culminating point of disaster to the royal arms ; while the concluding tableau represents him again at Whitehall in the closing stage of his career, leading to the scaffold. Nay more ; in addition to the observance of the unities of Time and Place, this Play follows the classic type by its observance of the third " dramatic unity " also—namely, that of Sentiment. Except (if it be an exception) the opening of the First Act, when the King is seen playing, but in sad fashion, with his children, the whole Drama relates to the continuous and augmenting disasters of the "royal martyr." The element of *relief*, by variety of emotion and humorous contrast, so systematically employed by Shakespeare, is wholly absent—there is not a laugh in the whole Play. There is no appliance of Music, by which the unity, if not monotony, of Sentiment was systematically relieved in the old Greek Tragedies. On the other hand, there is more dramatic incident and more work for the Actor than was usual in the Greek Dramas.

Mr Wills's latest Play, "Jane Shore," differs widely from the Greek Drama in some respects, yet in another resembles it even more closely than "Charles I." does. It differs as regards the unities of Time and Place, for it has seven scenes, six of these being in distinct localities; although it is obvious that the Author has done his utmost to observe these unities, and does so to an extent by no means usual in the English Drama. Nevertheless, on witnessing "Jane Shore," I *felt* the resemblance which the work bears to a Greek Play even more strikingly than when witnessing "Charles I." The unity of Sentiment is perfect; and despite the greater changes of scene, I felt as if I were witnessing the sorrows of Hecuba or Antigone. There is nothing more trying than to witness a monotony of sorrow and calamity on the stage (though not in the Opera, to which the Greek Tragedies were akin); and the popularity of this Play speaks volumes alike for the dramatic skill and poetic power of the Author, and for the culture or artistic appreciation of the audience. The house was full in every part; and I confess that it was with some surprise, and also with pleasant pride, that I saw unmistakably that such a drama was thoroughly appreciated even by "the gods."

For a good many years the Poetic Drama had fallen into the shade, almost into disrepute. In this, however, it only shared the fate of Poetry in general. The grand cycle of revived poetic feeling which accompanied the Great War, and which produced or was represented by a galaxy of our greatest poets—Burns, Byron, Scott, Coleridge, Southey, Shelley, Keates, Moore, Campbell, and Wordsworth—had died away; and after Lord Lytton's "Richelieu," and his still finer work the "Lady of Lyons," there was a total cessation of the Poetic Drama. The "high drama" disappeared, and it came to be thought that Poetry on the stage was a mistake. It is now clearly demonstrated—and the fact is a most gratifying one as regards the quality of our theatrical audiences—that this belief was all wrong, or else there has been a sudden and happy return to higher sentiment. Mr Wills boldly revived the Poetic Drama, and instead of emptying the theatre, he has filled it, and found admiring audiences. Poetry, as of yore, is recognised as the highest form of speech—the language most suitable for all high event and emotion, and in which these strike home most powerfully to the heart: and this judgment is given not only by the cultured occupants of the stalls, but by the broad heart of humanity which beats in the gallery—and in such a question the verdict of the latter class is even more valuable than that of the former.

These two Plays of Mr Wills's also serve to illustrate a feature of the Greek Drama, and a condition requisite for the successful adoption of its peculiar structure, to which I previously alluded—namely, that the Story or subject-matter of the drama must, in its broad outlines at least, be familiar to the audience. It is impossible to combine Simplicity of Scene with Novelty of story, or dramatic creation ; but this becomes attainable when the story or legend is familiar to the audience, whose knowledge of the subject renders unnecessary the representation of the minor events and connecting links, and thereby allows of the dramatist massing and concentrating the events in single scenes, representing the story at its culminating points, and lavishing his whole dramatic skill and poetic power upon these grand tableaux. Every one nowadays is familiar with the story of Charles I.; and hence it is in this Play that Mr Wills's dramatic skill has most fully succeeded in observing the unities of time and place—this Play, in fact, being as close a copy or reproduction (whether consciously or not upon the part of the author I cannot say) of the Greek Trilogy as can well be imagined on the Modern Stage, without an actual revival of the Greek Theatre with its musical and other accessories. In "Jane Shore" the story is by no means so familiar to the audience ; moreover, in this Play Mr Wills—wisely and well, I think—deviates from History, giving play to dramatic creation, and partial Novelty of story. But exactly in proportion as he does this, he has to sacrifice Simplicity of Scene. In the First Act, he is able to take a great deal for granted ; he gives no preliminary description of who his heroine is, or how she came to be there—for his audience know it beforehand sufficiently well. But the moment he comes to incidents of his own creation (and it would be the same if the incidents, although historically true, were unknown to his audience at large) he has to say good-bye to Simplicity of Scene, and follow the ordinary course of the Modern Drama in disregarding the unities of time and place.

One more remark as to Mr Wills's "Charles I." Although in its construction it far more closely resembles the old Greek Tragedies, in their form of the Trilogy, than any other work belonging to our modern Serious Drama, it also exemplifies the difficulties attendant upon this form or type of the Drama, and clearly illustrates the statement which I have previously made, that when a conflict of Realism arises between the Eye and the Mind, the compromise ought to go, as far as possible, in favour of the Eye. For example, in this Play it is indispensable that the cause of the fatal treachery of Lord March to his Royal Master, whose favourite he was, should be made briefly but clearly intelligible, and still more the actual form which this treachery took in deciding the issue of the battle against the King. Accordingly this is done by the interview between Ireton and March in the middle of Act III.; but rather than break the Simplicity of Scene, this interview is made to take place in the Royal camp, where it was not possible for Ireton to be—nay, actually beside the tent where the Queen is reposing! Nothing more impossible could well be represented;

nevertheless, this violation of all probability is not only artistically justifiable, but practically successful. The interview is a short one—only 30 lines,—which is an important condition of its success; and Ireton passes from view before, or almost before, the Mind of the audience takes note of the incongruity. When witnessing the Play, it seemed to me, as Ireton and March appeared beside the tent of the sleeping Queen, somewhat as if it were a ghost-scene, or rather the representation or revelation of a distant event seen by clairvoyance: but before I could well shape my thoughts or reflections upon what was passing before my eyes, the interview was over, and the impossible intruder had disappeared. Hence, I repeat, the briefness of this impossible scene is one of the causes, and I believe the chief condition, of the practical success of this or any suchlike violation of the realism of Event for the sake of maintaining the realism of Scene. It is a successful compromise in favour of the Eye, but which necessarily involves a discord,— and discords, whether in Music or in any other Art, must be brief. On the other hand, in the Play as printed for the general reader, this impossible interview, short though it be, is felt as absurd, an outrage on the common-sense of the reader.

I make this remark not in derogation from, but in em- phatic approval of, Mr Wills's work. A perfected Theatre —unless we are to return to the pure Greek type of drama —demands, in some cases at least, a compromise between the Eye and the Mind, or of the Eye *plus* Mind relative to the Mind alone; and the canons of criticism differ, I do not say widely, yet considerably, according as they are applied to a Play *acted*, or *read*—to a drama as a purely literary work, meant to be enjoyed by the reading public, or as represented on the Stage. The Mind, the reader, requires no compromises,—the more clearly and perfectly the drama is developed, the better. In the perusal of a drama (as of any other literary work), any incongruity or impossibility of Event is felt with full and unmitigated force as a violation of Realism ; because there is no counter-illusion of realism such as is maintained on the Stage to the Eye by Simplicity of Scene, which is at least an *apparent* maintenance of the unities of Time and Place, so important for theatrical illusion.

The old Greek Plays are now being revived at times on the British Stage,—a course which, in any form, would have been impracticable but for the recent perfecting of the Theatre. But they will never prove successful as popular theatrical entertainments. These old dramas turn upon sentiments and social or religious usages which are wholly obsolete. This is the grand and insurmountable difficulty : the audience cannot sympathise with them. I think it not improbable that one or two modern dramas will be composed upon the model of the Athenian drama, because this kind of Play is peculiarly fitted to employ all the finest appliances of the Theatre, as well as to suit a highly-cultured audience. But any such revival of the Greek model will require a richer employment of language, and still more, a different kind of acting, from what at present prevails. The Greek Plays, apart from their choral songs and music, were recited, rather than acted, dramas. All the exciting events, which a modern dramatist carefully presents as special elements of attraction to the audience, took place off the Stage. The Greek Drama, in fact, consists of two elements— namely, a *recital* in grand and picturesque language of the stirring events connected with the piece; and secondly, and chiefly, in the expression of the Emotions connected with these events, in the grandest and most beautiful form which human speech and music can assume. But of acting, in our sense of the word, there was little or none. Hence, together with the choral music and "emotional dance" (if we may so call it), the charm of the Greek Drama consisted in splendour and beauty of language,— applied, partly, to a grand recital of the events, but still more to the expression of Emotion. Poetry and grand elocution, interspersed with music, were intrusted to accomplish what Music alone does in the modern Opera and Oratorio.

The recent representation of the "Alcestis" at the Crystal Palace serves to show how these points have been overlooked, and how different are the qualities required of the actor in the old Greek Drama from those which distinguish the English Stage at the present time. Poetic drama has been so long out of vogue that the present generation of actors, as a class, are strangers to it; while their style of acting is equally alien to it. As the critic of the 'Daily News' remarked: "English acting tends essentially to a [kind of] realism which is directly opposed to the character of an ancient drama. Even the spurious classicism of the French stage has derived a sustaining power from

the circumstance that French actors of the best class have
always been trained in a school which aims at investing
the poetical drama with an ideal character. The per-
formers at the Crystal Palace, on the contrary, not only
strive to act as they conceive that *average* humanity would
conduct itself in the circumstances in which they are
placed, but they endeavour to speak Dr Potter's lines as
if their rhythmical and rhetorical character were features
not to be indicated but rather to be got over as best may
be, in deference to the undeniable truth that average persons do not use blank verse, or systematically employ
figures of speech in conveying to others their views and
sentiments. One of Mr Boucicault's domestic pieces, with
a fire in the third act, could not be further removed than
is the whole performance from the imaginative vein. This,
however, is chiefly felt in the delivery of the lines. The
truth is, that among us the art of poetical declamation is
scarcely cultivated at all. Any one who has heard a refined French actress—say, for example, Madame Favart
—deliver verse, and has marked the appropriate varieties
of tone, the subtle shades of emphasis, the exquisite art
of dropping, as it were, into the ear of the audience a sig-
nificant word just where it seems to have been expected,
and this without failing to indicate the measured march
of the poet's Alexandrines, will perceive at once that
there is at least one very important condition almost
always wanting in the performance of a poetical play on
our stage. All this may have little affinity with Greek
notions of rhythm and music; but it serves at least to attune
the mind of the audience to the spirit of the ideal drama."

Comedy, especially of the lighter sort, is at present the grand success of the English stage; and it is Comedy, with its minute attention to realism, which has given its style to our modern acting. Indeed, in playing Shakespeare's characters, Mr Fechter set a bad and mistaken example by adopting this style to a considerable extent even in the grand and poetic drama: he sought to represent *average* humanity while acting characters of a grand and more or less ideal type. He sought to "play down" to his audience,—to represent Shakespeare's heroes as if cast in no higher mould than the occupants of the pit and stalls. This was a poor compliment to his audience; it was to ignore the fact that (despite the *nil admirari* precept of Horace and Byron) Admiration, the sense of beauty and grandeur, of what is higher than one's self, is one of the most pleasurable as well as elevating of human faculties and emotions. What could be meaner and pettier than where Fechter made Othello, in his grand rage and agony when about to murder Desdemona, turn to look at his own face in a mirror, as if to say—"Ah, I see!—it is my black face has done it all: she prefers a lover of her own complexion!" The old school of great Tragedians—Kemble, Siddons, and others—could never have perpetrated such an indignity to Shakespeare; or, I may say, to human nature. Moreover, these great actors of the older time loved and appreciated Verse, and could speak it naturally and grandly. So, too, with the French Tragedians, who can deliver their rhymed verse with a charm and expressiveness which, as the 'Daily News' critic says truly, is at present a lost art on this side the

Channel. It will be vain to revive the Greek dramas until the art of reciting lofty and beautiful verse dramatically is regained. And not to be able to do this is simply a confession that speech in its highest and most lovely form is beyond the power of our actors.

A critic once replied to an admirer of Fechter's acting in tragedy on the ground of its "naturalness" by the remark, "Natural,—but according to *whose* nature?" Certainly not that of Lear, Hamlet, or Othello. So likewise in regard to Language. It is true that average men and women do not talk in verse: but, for that matter, neither do they talk in the brilliant dialogue of Sheridan, or in the clever and sparkling witticisms which abound in comedies even of a lower class. Neither do they think, feel, and act like the higher characters of the Drama; but none the less, perhaps the more, do they admire the representation of humanity in its loftier and more lovely forms; and the more nearly an individual possesses the higher capacities of human nature, the more nearly, under appropriate circumstances, would he speak and act like the characters whose portrayal he admires. He admires them because their speech and action are *natural* in the personages and circumstances created by the dramatic poet. Ordinary men are not six feet high, nor walk like Weston, nor speak like Gladstone; neither are ordinary women beautiful as Mary Queen of Scots or the Princess of Wales; nor can they sing like Patti or Tietjens. But no one would say that these gifts are not natural in their favoured possessors. The mistake arises from confounding what is ordinary or usual with what is natural,—or rather, of restricting what is *natural* to what is *ordinary*. It is not usual for a man to be able to throw a heavy iron bar thirty yards ; but certainly such an act is natural enough to a man who can do it.

Just so is it with Language. Men with a lively sensibility, and with the poetic faculty, when stirred by adequate circumstance will express their feelings or ideas in verse as naturally as ordinary men will do in prose. And rhythmic speech goes as naturally with lofty thought and action in the Drama as Dickens's clever and amusing Cockney-dialogue goes with Sam Weller. The former may be less *usual* than the latter, but it is equally *natural.* The piano, when struck, yields sounds accordant to the notes which it possesses : the common piano has not the wide reach of the "grand"—it neither goes so low nor so high : but if the notes, the capacity, be there, the wider musical range, the full depths of the bass and the high brilliance of the treble are as natural to the grander instrument as is their absence in the smaller one.

The whole *rationale* and true naturalness of Poetry consists in this, that when the Mind is excited and elevated by lofty or beautiful Emotion, speech rises naturally into rhythmic prose (witness the finest passages of Oratory), and next into the rich and various rhythmic cadences of "blank verse ;" and finally—especially when the exciting Emotion belongs to Love, tenderness, or the Beautiful generally—it with equal naturalness culminates in rhymed verse, in rhythm capped by the further beauty of Rhyme. Rhymed verse, with its melodious consonances, or Poetry in its highest form, is the perfection of melodious Speech.

Hence, by universal accord, it is adopted in Songs, Odes, and other forms of Poetry in which a perfection of melodious language is required,—where speech is elevated to the highest point of Beauty. Every kind of high thought or emotion can be effectively expressed in rhymed verse; indeed, as Shakespeare shows, it can be wedded even to fierce and energetic action, lending additional force to the lines: but its harmony of sound is peculiarly accordant with the tender passions, and with calm, lofty thought. Rhyme binds successive lines melodiously together; and this melodious consonance and linking of lines is most suitable where the emotion is smooth and sustained—as in passages of stately grandeur, tenderness, or love— whereby the development of the one sentiment in its various phases or variations is linked and rounded by a unity or harmony of melodious sound.

Shakespeare is undoubtedly the highest dramatic genius the world has ever produced; and what is the example which he gives in this matter? No other modern dramatist employs language in such full variety. He employs speech in each and all of its phases or different gradations —from the lowest to the highest; his language varying, free and unconfined, solely and perfectly in accordance with the changing mood or theme. Prose, blank verse, and rhyme—he employs them all; not merely in the same drama, but in the same scene—sometimes even in the same speech; passing to and fro from one to the other, often by rapid transition, but with constant appropriateness and naturalness. Obviously he did not say to himself (no great author does), "Here I shall use prose, here

I shall speak in verse, here I shall make the verse blossom into rhyme." He did it naturally: as the subject or emotion varied, so did his own mood and emotions, spontaneously finding voice in accordant language.

The Greek Drama represented language *uniformly* in its highest shape. Its peculiar structure not only permitted, but was expressly designed for, the employment of speech in its highest and most beautiful forms,—indeed this was the primest object and feature of the glorious dramatic works of the Athenian stage. All tragic and energetic *action* for which the melody of Verse was unsuitable, took place off the Stage, and was represented only by recital, —the language descriptive of the events naturally assuming quite a different form from what it would necessarily have borne had it been the utterances of men actually engaged in those events. It was but the *reflection* of those events that had to be expressed, together with the *emotions* of the "situation" as represented on the stage; and thus the language of the actors, the voice of emotion, could rise without obstruction into the highest forms of stately and melodious speech. The subject-matter of the drama was uniformly solemn (although the Chorus, especially in the plays of Euripides, sometimes breaks into sunny bursts of description), but the modulations or "variations" (to speak musically) of the prevailing sentiment were expressed in various and elaborate verse. What is more, although rhyme was dispensed with in Greek verse — the full vowel-sounds of that language yielding a richness of melody unattainable in modern languages,—a German critic has pointed out that rhyme

is employed occasionally in the Greek Tragedies (sometimes in upwards of a hundred places in a single drama),
deliberately and by direct purpose on the part of the
author.   Indeed, apart from special reasons, it is incon-
ceivable that these numerous instances of rhyme could
have occurred save intentionally in such works, wherein
the Verse, and the artistic employment of language in its
highest forms, was the primest study of the author and
the chief attraction to the audience.   There is also a well-
known instance in Horace's Odes, where he employs
rhyme to heighten the melody of the Greek metre which
he is using—viz., the Sapphic and Adonian—in his tender
lines to Lalage :—

> " Pone me pigris ubi nulla campis
> Arbor æstivâ recreatur aurâ."

In the first of these two lines we have simple rhyme
added to and accentuating the rhythm ; and in the second
line, the rhyme is actually manifold,—the full-sounding a
is heard not merely in the major cadences, at the middle
and end of the line, but also in the opening syllable, and
again in the eighth. The rhythm, in fact, besides being
the most melodious of classic metres, is as full of rhyme
as is possible, or as any line in Moore's 'Melodies,' or of
any other of the pre-eminently lyrical and fluently rhym-
ing poets of Ireland.

Rhymed verse is systematically employed by the
" classic " dramatists of France and Italy.   In their
plays, as in the Greek drama, splendour of language,
expressive of lofty thought, heroic sentiment, and ten-

derness of emotion, is the special charm, rather than the representation of *action*. Also, as in the Greek drama, the works of the French dramatists preserve a uniformity of serious sentiment; and thus, to a certain extent, the stately sonorousness of the rhymed Alexandrine verse is not unsuitable; although, both in beauty and appropriateness, it falls short of, and looks tame beside, the varying verse of the Athenian Drama.

In the Shakespearian Drama we enter an essentially different world of scenic life. His Plays are full of vivid *action*,—the most tragic and tumultuous events are presented, fully acted, on the stage; and further, instead of the "classic" unity of sentiment, we find systematic Variety and the most abrupt contrasts. Even in his tragedies—the parallels of the Greek Drama and the classic drama of France—the whole range of human life is represented, the whole gamut of sentiment is sounded. The voice of vulgar humanity, of the courtly wit, or even of the buffoon, is heard as a contrast, relief, and by-play amid the most tragic events and in dialogue and monologue of loftiest emotion and reflection. And the language varies accordingly. In not a single one even of his tragedies does he adhere to a uniformity of language. Indeed, in each and all of them, he employs every gradation of speech, from the language of the peasant up to that of ideal humanity under the sway of the loftiest or loveliest emotions. And he does so with a variety and rapid vicissitude — a bold *naturalness* — that no other English dramatist has equalled, or indeed approached. Putting aside his prose-dialogue, let us consider his Verse.

The blank verse, or unrhymed metre, of Shakespeare is widely different from that of Milton. It is the verse of the drama, not of the Poem. Instead of the organ-like swell and sustained cadences of Milton, we find a lively motion in the verse, with the quick transitions and abrupt pauses appropriate to a dialogue directly wedded to dramatic action. It is only, or almost only, in his monologues, or where his characters *reflect* while the action is suspended, that Shakespeare employs "blank verse" of the true type. True blank verse, as employed in a different style by Milton and Tennyson, must always be written in lines of ten syllables, and must be spoken· accordingly. Various as are the cadences of blank verse, —sometimes, as in Milton, the major rhythm extends in a continuous roll over half-a-dozen successive lines, with minor cadences between—there is always a cadence, a cæsural pause, of some degree after every tenth syllable: and this is indispensable to the true blank verse of poetry —it is this which "differentiates" it from rhythmic prose, —or rather, I should say, from rhythmic and unrhymed language in other form than blank verse; for this rhythmic language is *capable* of melody almost equal to that of blank verse, although different in kind,—possessing less sonorousness, but more flexibility and power of varied expression.

This rhythmic language appears to me highly suitable for the main body of a heroic or poetic drama; because it is by far the most flexible of all forms of language. It can be made to pass readily, and without abrupt transition, into prose dialogue, as well as suitably to alternate

or intermingle with it; or it can rise into rhymed verse,
—the rhymes falling upon and capping the free-moving
major cadences; or pass into true blank verse, with its
organ-like roll,—or again into the rhymed heroic couplet.

This form of speech is largely employed in Shakespeare's dramas. Although written in lines of ten syllables, his verse abounds in short or broken lines; also
the lines end with exceeding frequency in the colloquial
double-syllable; also in thousands of instances there is
no cæsural pause at all at the end of the decasyllabic
lines,—and these would be fatal defects in true blank
verse, whether of the Miltonian or Tennysonian kind.
But these are not defects at all in Shakespeare's verse,
and they can only appear to be so to those who imagine
that Shakespeare always meant to write pure blank
verse.

The short, and apparently broken, lines are quite different from the *unfinished* lines found here and there in
Virgil's 'Æneid:' they are, really, employments of what I
may call the free rhythmic verse. Shakespeare, too, sometimes combines prose with blank verse—or verse, even
rhyme, with prose—*in the same speech*, in a manner that
used to puzzle commentators, who could not understand
this gradation of speech, and who strove to scan the
interjected prose into verse, or to reduce the verse into
prose. Ordinary instances of this kind are too abundant
to need illustration; but here is a very curious one from
Act i. scene 2 of the "Merchant of Venice," where Portia,
conversing with Nerissa and Servant in prose, passes in
the closing sentences of her last speech or remarks (which

also close the scene) from prose into verse of a very loose-
jointed kind, but capped by rhyme :—

"*Portia*. If I could bid the fifth [wooer] welcome with so good a
heart as I can bid the other four farewell, I should be glad of his
approach : if he have the condition of a saint and the complexion of
a devil, I had rather he should shrive me than wive me.
Come, Nerissa !   Sirrah, go before.
Whiles we shut the gates upon one wooer, another knocks at the
    door."

But what I especially desire to call attention to is
Shakespeare's employment of *rhymed* verse,—very copi-
ously, and in a manner totally different from that of our
other dramatists.   Shakespeare's employment of rhymed
verse may be classed under three heads.   Firstly, there
are the highly imaginative or supernatural passages, like
the Witch Scenes in " Macbeth," where the supernatural
characters speak in rhymed verse of various kinds ; also in
the Play within a Play of the actors in " Hamlet ;" and
also generally, I might say universally, in all scrolls and
suchlike documents, from the contents of the caskets in
the " Merchant of Venice " down to the paper picked up
on the eve of the battle, in " Richard III."—

" Jockey of Norfolk, be not too bold,
    For Dickon thy master is bought and sold."

Secondly, there are the passages where rhyme is used
to emphasise the utterances of the speaker.   Here the
verse rises into the rhymed couplet, usually at the close
of the speech, finely rounding it off, and giving to the
sentiment a power and force otherwise unattainable.

The words are winged by the rhyme, and the couplet goes home to its mark like a rifled projectile from a double-charged gun. Nearly all the most striking of Shakespeare's lines, and those which he evidently meant to be striking, are rhymed : *e.g.*—

> " The Play's the thing,
> Wherein I'll catch the conscience of the King ! "

Or Macbeth's awful exclamation when the bell rings to announce that all is ready for him to carry out his deed of blood—

> " Hear it not, Duncan ; for it is a knell
> That summons thee to heaven or to hell ! "

These rhymed couplets, sometimes even quatrains, abound in Shakespeare's tragedies, and at the end of a scene they are so frequent as to be usual. Take, for instance, the concluding Act of " Macbeth," where the action and emotion are rising to their culminating point :—

SCENE 1.

Doctor. " And still keep eyes upon her. So, good night :
My mind she has mated, and amazed my sight."

SCENE 2.

Lennox.   " Or so much as it needs,
To dew the sovereign flower and drown the weeds."

> [*Exeunt.*

SCENE 3.

Macbeth. " The mind I sway by and the heart I bear
Shall never sag with doubt nor shake with fear."

Macbeth. " I will not be afraid of death and bane,
Till Birnam forest come to Dunsinane.
Doct. (*aside*). Were I from Dunsinane away and clear,
Profit again should hardly draw me here."   [*Exeunt*

SCENE 4.

Siward.   "The time approaches
That will with due decision let us know
What we shall say we have and what we owe.
Thoughts speculative their unsure hopes relate,
But certain issue strokes must arbitrate :
Towards which advance the war ! "   [*Exeunt.*

SCENE 5.

Macbeth.   " Arm, arm, and out !
If this which he avouches doth appear,
There is nor flying hence nor tarrying here.
I 'gin to be aweary of the sun,
And wish the estate o' the world were now undone.
Ring the alarum-bell !   Blow, wind ! come, wrack !
At least we'll die with harness on our back."   [*Exeunt.*

What a storm of martial sound there is in these two
last lines !—yet what would the words be if not cast in
the rhymed verse?

SCENE 6.

Macduff. " Make all our trumpets speak ; give them all breath,
Those clamorous harbingers of blood and death."
                                                    [*Exeunt.*
SCENE 8.

Macbeth.   " Lay on, Macduff ;
And damn'd be him that first cries, *Hold, enough !* " [*Exeunt.*

And the tragedy closes with King Malcolm's address
to his lieges, which he ends in rhyme as the curtain falls.

Malcolm.   " This, and what needful else
That calls upon us, by the grace of Grace,
We will perform in measure, time, and place ;
So, thanks to all at once and to each one,
Whom we invite to see us crown'd at Scone."

Thirdly, Shakespeare uses rhyme in entire speeches, sometimes in whole scenes, as in " Romeo and Juliet," the Casket-scene in the "Merchant of Venice," and other plays. Witness especially "Henry VI.," Act iv., where rhymed verse, in the form of the heroic couplet, is employed throughout three successive scenes, where brave old Talbot and his gallant boy meet after seven years' absence, only to fight and die together in the lost battle at Bourdeaux,—ending with the famous old General's dying words—

> " Come, come, and lay him in his father's arms ;
> My spirit can no longer bear these harms.
> Soldiers, adieu ! I have what I would have,
> Now my old arms are young John Talbot's grave."

Would any blank verse equal the rhymed couplet in doing justice to the lofty pathos and heroism of these scenes ? I trow not.

Lastly, as to the employment of Music in connection with highly poetic dialogue, and especially with rhymed verse. The two naturally go together. Rhymed verse is poetry in its most beautiful form, and by universal accord music is most appropriate to it. Of itself, it is more highly charged with music than any other form of speech or verse : to the *melody* of the rhythm there is superadded the *harmony* of the consonant rhymes,—it is language beautified and surcharged with music.

Despite the fact that the artistic appliances of the Theatre were of the most meagre description in his day, Shakespeare in several instances expressly enjoins the employment of music in connection with his verse-passages,

and especially where he uses rhyme. The Witch-scene in
the 4th Act of "Macbeth" is hardly a case in point; for
there, although rhyme is employed, there is no beauty of
language to be sustained or heightened,—the chief pur-
poses of the music being in connection with the spectacular
effect, and, specially, to raise the emotions of the audience
so as to bring them into sympathy with the *supernatural-
ness* of the scene. The earliest representations which I
witnessed of "Macbeth" were devoid of music, and the
grand Witch-scene, baldly presented, looked more absurd
than impressive; but when I saw the same scene, accompanied with Locke's music, I felt at once how vastly the
effect was heightened, and also the *naturalness* (if I may
so call it), of the supernatural event portrayed. But a
true and perfect example of Shakespeare's use of music
to heighten the effect of beautiful poetry is to be seen in
the Casket-scene in the "Merchant of Venice" (Act iii.
scene 2), where high blank verse, rhymed verse, and lyric
song are all employed. Portia says, "Let music sound
while he doth make his choice." Then a song is sung,
"Tell me where is Fancy bred;" and also there is the
stage-direction, "Music, whilst Bassanio comments on the
caskets to himself."

While Shakespeare in the rich variety of his language is
a dramatic model for all time—in this respect rivalling
or surpassing the finest of the Athenian tragedies, and
quite unequalled by any dramatist of modern times,—
the construction of his plays has become defective with
the growth of the Theatre, while the Greek model is being
revived, or at least its *principle* is being preferred, and ere

long will be more and more observed. Apart from the circumstance that our Theatre, possessing the fullest artistic
accessories and appliances, now *permits* of the adequate
representation of drama of the Greek type, is there not a
change in the condition and tastes of modern audiences
which points in the same direction ? The æsthetic Greeks
abjured the representation of tragic events upon the stage ;
they preferred to have them reflected and softened in the
mirror of poetic language. I have no doubt, also, that
the Greeks objected to representations of murder and
bodily cruelty on the stage as totally opposed to the illusion of reality—as a breach of illusion of the very worst
kind. They not only knew, but felt, that such representations were a sham ; and had such things been acted
on the stage, would not the cultured audience have simply
laughed at them ? The Athenians, like the modern
Parisians, were eminently quick-witted and alive to incongruity, and I believe that their exclusion of tragic
acts from the stage was due not nearly so much to their
"fine feelings," as to their keen sense of the absurdity
of such a performance. Is not a similar feeling arising
in modern audiences ? Our tastes are changing. In
Shakespeare's time, and until lately, the audience took
a lively interest in the most tragic events on the stage.
Their imagination was duller—probably they could not real-
ise the great events of the drama unless these were visibly
presented to them ; and undoubtedly they liked occasionally to sup full of horrors. Hence in Shakespeare's plays,
Banquo is murdered, Cæsar assassinated, Mercutio, Tybalt,
Cassio, and others killed in duels on the stage ; and the

death-combats of Macbeth and Macduff, and of Richard
III. and Richmond, used to be among the most attractive
parts of the performance of those great dramas—carefully
studied by the actor, and loudly applauded by the audience.

This was a rude taste, belonging to uncultured times ;
but now it is vanishing. In fact, I believe that it is
chiefly to this change of public taste that Tragedies have
almost gone out of fashion,—not (as most people believe) because they are tragedies, but because our tragedies, from those of Shakespeare downwards, have been
constructed on a principle now out of date. Theatrical
audiences have become critical in judgment, and also
more refined in sentiment. The characters on the
stage may rage or sorrow, be passionate in love, heroic
in sentiment, or lofty in reflection, to the fullest extent,
truthfully portrayed,—all this is *natural*, though it be
human nature in its higher types,—and the audience
will admire and applaud. But "when the brains are out,
there is an end o't." The killing of a man on the stage
is a breach of realism of the most violent kind ; or, so
far as any impression of reality is felt by the audience,
it is disagreeable or shocking. But I believe that the
prevailing sentiment of any audience of the better class,
when such tragic scenes are acted on the stage, is now that
of *sham*. And when Banquo is covered with wounds by
the bloody daggers of the 1st and 2d murderers, or when
Macbeth and Macduff, or Richard and Richmond, engage
in an elaborate death-combat, the audience are simply
inclined to laugh. Instead of the sensations of imaginative terror or horror, which earlier and uncultured

audiences experienced at the representation of these events in tragedies, it may safely be said that nowadays the more killings and murders in a piece, the more will the audience feel absurdity in the performance. They will laugh, or be tempted to laugh; and this is utterly fatal to a serious drama. The "illusion of reality"* is not only gone, but gives place to sensations fatal, above all others, to the effect of a dramatic performance.

Thus, the further we proceed in considering the matter, does it not appear more clearly than ever that the cultured Greeks had good grounds for their peculiar type of

---

* In the Athenian theatre it was a point of honour to make the production of a new drama excel its predecessors in the *mise en scène* (see Copleston's 'Æschylus' in Blackwoods' series of "Ancient Classics for English Readers"); and to show the perfection to which the Modern Theatre has attained, and the extent to which the "illusion of reality" is now carried, I cannot refrain from quoting from the newspapers an account of the production of Offenbach's new opera of "Dr Ox" at Paris :—"The costumes, which have been designed partly by M. Grévin and partly by M. Draner, are the most beautiful which have appeared since the Pompeian scene was composed in 'Le Roi Carotte.' Madame Judic's gipsy dress in the first act was copied by Grévin from Régnault's noble picture of Salomé; and even after this had been done, so anxious was the Management to reproduce the great painter's colours exactly, that the most expert dyers were employed to obtain stuff of the lively and delicate tints required. M. Draner has equally conscientiously designed the costumes confided to his artistic taste from historical engravings of the master-works of the old Dutch and Flemish schools. The *finale* of the second act, where more than a hundred persons appear together upon the stage, gives a correct notion of all that is most curious in the national attire of the Low Countries; and twelve of the ballet girls wear a faithful pattern of the Marken Islanders' dress, which is not unlike a Russian costume. In like manner, the Scenery has been accurately painted from photographs taken in Holland for the purpose; and M. Mortier, who is an authentic subject of the King of the Netherlands, seems to have watched over the smallest effects of the scenery with eyes so patriotic and attentive that the result is such as to astonish even a Parisian audience accustomed to accuracy of detail."

dramatic construction? It seems to me, also, that the unpopularity of our existing *form* of Tragedies has been one cause of the supposed unpopularity of *poetic* dramas. It is only in our Tragedies that verse has been employed; and, the true cause of the waning popularity of these dramas being overlooked (viz., their antiquated construction), it was hastily inferred that it was their poetic style which had ceased to be appreciated. The success of Mr Wills's dramas has shown that this was a mistake,— as indeed the great popularity of Lord Lytton's "Lady of Lyons" has shown continuously; and so far from dramatic poetry going out of fashion, I believe that its attractions will be even more fully recognised as the Modern Theatre puts forth its complete and perfected powers for the entertainment of the cultured audiences of the present day. Dramatists must beware of Shakespeare as a model of Construction, but they may safely follow him (if they can) in the remarkable fulness and variety of his Poetry.

Also, if any one aspire to rival Shakespeare in his marvellous mastery of language—so terse and pregnant, so rich and picturesque—he need not seek to do so by copying the idioms of the sixteenth century, for the sake of giving a superficial resemblance to Shakespeare's style. This is to confound the perishable with the immortal,—it is to copy what would have had no place in Shakespeare's writings had he lived in the present age. These archaic expressions and style of language (which nowadays are a weak affectation), or recondite phraseology of any kind, are peculiarly out of place in the Drama, where the language, however lofty and beautiful, ought to be instantaneously intelligible, clear as light itself. Lord Lytton in all his Plays uses the language of his own time, and so ought every author to do, and especially every Dramatist.

Since these remarks were written, the Poet-Laureate has published his second drama,—a work in all respects worthy of his renown. In his first drama, "Queen Mary," Mr Tennyson followed the Shakespearian model, with its multiplicity of changes of scene; but in "Harold" he has obviously studied concentration of incident carefully,— although, partly owing to the story being unfamiliar to ordinary audiences, but chiefly owing to his mode of treatment, he has been compelled to represent the various stages of the heroic story separately, to a degree which renders unattainable the Simplicity of Scene and concentration of action which so remarkably characterise Mr Wills's " Charles I." There are eleven scenes in "Harold," ten of which are in different localities. But there is one feature in this work, and its grandest scene, which fully accords with what I have said as to the "new phase" and tendency of the Modern Drama. The Battle of Hastings and the death of Harold are treated almost exactly as they would have been in a Greek Tragedy. In "Macbeth," "Julius Cæsar," and other tragedies, Shakespeare presents the battles on the stage, following their course in a series of short scenes, where the characters are duly killed *coram populo*. Mr Tennyson banishes the battle from the stage, representing it only in *recital*, by a dialogue of onlookers. Moreover, he carries out this resemblance to the Athenian drama by heightening the effect of the scene by music and the chorus,—namely, by

the chanted song of the Monks, which alternates with the
dialogue. The descriptive and sympathetic dialogue, also,
is of the most vivid and impressive character; while the
nearness of the battle and the realism of the recital are
impressively supported by the shouts and war-cries of the
contending armies—the sturdy "Out! out!" of the English, and the fierce "Ha Rou!" of the Normans.

In "Harold," also—although in free play and richly
varied forms of language it falls short of Shakespeare's
style—we find a deviation from the monotony of blank
verse customary, and often so oppressive, in our English
tragedies of modern and post-Shakespearian date. Not
only is the Laureate's dramatic blank verse rightly different from the more melodious and perfect form which
it assumes in his Poems, but in various places of this
drama it passes visibly into that free rhythmic verse of
which I have previously spoken. Take the following instances (p. 134) :—

> *Harold.* "I die for England, then, who lived for England—
> What nobler?   Men must die.
> I cannot fall into a falser world—
> I have done no man wrong.   Tostig, poor brother,
> Art *thou* so anger'd?
> Fain had I kept thine earldom in thy hands," &c.

Here is a longer instance. Harold again *loquitur* (p.
109)—

> "Set forth our golden Dragon, let him flap
> The wings that beat down Wales!
> Advance our Standard of the Warrior,
> Dark among gems and gold; and thou, brave banner,
> Blaze like a night of fatal stars on those

Who read their doom and die.
Where lie the Norsemen? on the Derwent? ay,
At Stamford-bridge.
Morcar, collect thy men : Edwin, my friend—
Thou lingerest.—Gurth,—
Last night King Edward came to me in dreams—
The rosy face and long down-silvering beard—
He told me I should conquer :—
I am no woman to put faith in dreams."

Mr Tennyson apparently shrinks from the bold naturalness in the use of rhymed verse which characterises the
King of dramatists; but he employs both it and music
to a greater extent than is to be found in the tragedies
of other authors. Besides the impressive rhymed chant
of the monks, Edith, the heroine, on two occasions (of
course in soliloquy) gives voice to her tender emotions
in song. Shakespeare sometimes (with perfect naturalness, as I maintain—nor was Shakespeare likely to make
a mistake in this matter) makes the heroines of his
Tragedies speak in rhymed verse ; but, with the exception of the maniacal snatches of Ophelia, he never makes
them sing a song. The two songs in " Harold " are essentially, indeed peculiarly, songs,—so much so that they
cannot be *naturally* spoken — they must be sung. If
spoken, they would lose the charm which they are meant
to possess,—it would be like a painting without its colour.
The words are not particularly lyrical or beautiful of
themselves, but there is a wonderful latent charm in the
first of these warblings (as in most of the Laureate's
songs)—an underlying sentiment, which is meant to be
developed by music. The simple words, in fact, are as
expressly meant to be garlanded by music as the tree-

arcades of Italy are meant to be festooned by the graceful foliage and blooming fruit-clusters of the vine. These
songs in " Harold, a Tragedy," are a bold innovation ; but
no absolute rule can be laid down for the details of dramatic treatment, which so vary with mood, sentiment, and
circumstance, that what is appropriate or inappropriate in
one place may possibly be the reverse in another.

Be this as it may, the case stands thus. In " Harold,"
our newest tragedy, and by our greatest poet, we now
have the Greek principle of *recital* of tragic events, instead
of *acting* them,—this recital, moreover, being accompanied
by what is in fact the Chorus and Music of the Athenian
drama : music and rhymed verse being still further employed in the songs of the heroine ; while the customary
monotony of our dramatic poetry is also relieved by the
occasional employment of the free rhythmic verse.

There are no themes more natural or more tempting for
the Dramatic Muse—for Tragedies, or for the serious and
poetic Drama generally—as grand events of History :
but these subjects have a danger peculiar to themselves,
and one which, if I may venture to say so, the Laureate
has not wholly avoided in his " Harold." The dramatist
must not chiefly write History ; the interest of his work
must be of a personal, not of an historical kind. Grand
as may be the epoch to which the drama relates, it is
not upon an interest of this kind that a successful play
can rely, but upon the sentiments and passions of the
individual characters, — not upon the grand events of
the epoch, but upon the mode in which these influence
the actors in the story. In the Greek Tragedies, as I

have repeatedly said, it is not upon a portrayal of the
Events, but of the passions and emotions excited by the
Events, that the poet-authors employed their high powers,
and which supply the elements of interest to the audience.

A grand epoch in its purely historical aspect may be
fitly and successfully made the theme of a Poem: indeed
a Poem, as the highest form of language, may narrate
such events as faithfully, and also more grandly and
beautifully than History,—necessarily with a loss of many
of the minor facts, but with a grander sweep and with
a more vivid presentment of the aspect of the times.
But the case is otherwise with the Drama—and indeed
with the Novel also. And by reference to the Novel,
I can perhaps best describe the difference. Take, for
example, the Historical Novels of two of the greatest
masters in that domain of imagination, Scott and Bulwer-
Lytton. The finest of Bulwer-Lytton's historical novels
is 'The Last Days of Pompeii.' Why? Because in it he
was least tied, and overpowered, by History. In fact, in
that novel there was no History to be kept in mind at all.
But when we come to his other works of this class, say his
'Harold,' the work of art is far inferior. It is *first* History,
and only secondarily a Novel. His mode of treatment is
to represent the Period, the Events ; and the imaginative
and personal elements, although the largest in bulk, are
merely interjected embellishments of the historical theme.
The History overpowers him—as it must do any author
who adopts the same method of treatment. On the other
hand, look at Scott. I have seen it remarked that Scott
never selected as his heroes the grand historical person-

ages of the time in which his tale is laid—not even in his Poems; for these he made, and desired to make, poetic Novels. And it was said he did this from a reluctance or inadequacy for the task of portraying those great personages. This criticism not only does injustice to Scott (about which I do not here concern myself), but proceeds from an entire mistake of Scott's plan of work. No man could better delineate great historic personages than Scott; and briefly as they appear on his scenes, he gives to them a more vivid and not less accurate presentment than perhaps even the best Historian has done. What can be more graphic and realistic than his sketches of the Lion-Heart of England; the wily, cowardly Louis XI. of France; or the chivalrous Saladin?

The true explanation of Scott's method was (though most probably he did not reason the matter at all, but worked by the instinct of his genius) the fundamental difference between the Novel and History. It is a low— certainly it is not the highest—form of the Novel which simply embellishes History. Scott's novels were imaginative creations, laid in great periods, but not describing them. The grand personages of the Period look in upon his story, and the grand aspect and movement of the Period overhang it like a sky: but the story follows its own course, and the *interest* is essentially of a personal, not of an historical kind—indeed, the most interesting incidents and personages are purely fictitious. In the Drama this mode of treatment is at least as imperative or desirable as in the Novel. When the Drama concerns itself with depicting the Period or Events, it is at once overpowered by History; and the characters, instead of moving by free spontaneous life, become little more than automata, giving voice to the events, and their speeches are History in dialogue. They are "lay-figures," exciting little interest, because we know the history, and that they must act in obedience to it. In this way the great charm of the Drama is lost,—for the interest of the Drama ought to be purely personal, based upon the emotions of the individual, not on the course of the Time. It is Human Nature that we primarily want, not History. Look at Shakespeare's historical dramas. He follows History much more closely than Scott did in his Novels; but in those days, when books were few and reading rare with the public, there was a value and an attraction in the representation on the stage of the grand events of our national history such as are non-existent now,—much in the same way as the old Scripture Plays had both a charm and a value when the Bible was a "sealed book" to the multitude, which do not pertain to them now. But even in the historical dramas of Shakespeare, nearly one-half consists of pure bye-play, with imaginary characters (like Pistol, Nym, and Bardolph), and usually of a comic description,—an element of variety and relief, which our King of dramatists never overlooked. The chief element of interest is not that pertaining to the events, but to the portrayal of human nature in its higher forms in connection with those events—the inner life of the characters, their secret thoughts, and their bye-play of action, portrayed by the genius of Shakespeare. History cannot tell us what Cæsar thought and spoke, or the

moralisings of Cato; and in "Richard III." the interest
is created chiefly by the imagination of the author, in
divining and depicting the inner life and private personality of the Hunchback Tyrant. Moreover, as works of
art, these historical Plays do not equal "Othello," "Hamlet," "Macbeth," "The Merchant of Venice," "Romeo and
Juliet," and the "Tempest," where History is wholly absent,
and even legend (if any) is a mere outline, and where the
subject is purely a development of Human Nature in its
eternal forms, but in its higher types, and under the
pressure of exciting incidents, as portrayed by a great
Poet and the greatest seer of the human heart that ever
lived.

The Poem can deal most successfully even with pure
History,—and still more with the dim but often mar-
vellously attractive domain of national legend. But
in the Drama it is always perilous to make the main
line of action (in such case it cannot be called a "plot")
coincide and progress along with the course of historical events; and when this is done, the interest ought
to lie in matters which are not History, though bor-
rowing from it their general complexion. Lord Lytton's
"Richelieu" is not so fine a Play as his "Lady of Lyons,"
but even in "Richelieu," the interest lies in depicting the
complex personality and inner life of the great Minister
under wholly fictitious circumstances—in an imaginary
microcosm, lying within and taking its colour from the
historical macrocosm, but composed chiefly of personages
and wholly of incidents of which History knows nothing.
History, in short, makes a grand groundwork for the

Drama ; but if it supplies both the figures and chief incidents of the dramatic picture, only the highest dramatic
genius can prevent the characters becoming uninteresting
automata,—lay-figures speaking History in dialogue. And
here again I must praise Mr Wills's "Charles I." as a
model of construction for the pure Historical Drama,—his
theme of interest being not the Events, but the emotions
and development of character excited by the events,—
History being mirrored in his scenes rather than acted,—
all his scenes, in truth, belonging to the bye-play of History, but quite beyond its ken ; and thus the characters
are free to show, and do show, the spontaneity of life and
action which is indispensable for dramatic interest. At
the same time it must be said that his strict observance of
the " unity of sentiment" cannot be accepted as a general
rule, however imperative it may be in the pure Greek
Drama, with its musical and other elements of relief.

Although I indulge in this Preface—which, beyond my
purpose, has grown into an Essay—tempted thereto by
the new phase which appears to me to be coming over
the Modern Drama, alike in its construction and in
theatrical representation, and which I think will progress,
—I beg it to be understood that these foregoing remarks
have little or no connection with this Drama of mine,
for which a lengthy exordium were out of place, and
which was written full seven years ago, at a time when
the change in question had not attracted my attention

and indeed had hardly become observable. "Robespierre" belongs to the Modern or Romantic school of drama, not to the Classic,—relying for interest mainly upon novelty of story and incident.   At the same time I think it accords with the revived perfection of Theatrical representation by introducing along with the dialogue and dramatic action the enrichment of Music, in the choruses, as well as the Spectacular effects and the Ballet.

With regard to those parts of the dialogue in which rhythm is heightened or further accentuated by rhyme, I shall not, I hope need not, quote high authorities or adduce arguments.   I shall only state the fact, for what it is worth, that in those places the rhymed verse came naturally to me.   It was written spontaneously, and I am confident it can be spoken naturally.

"Robespierre" cannot boast of the Simplicity of Scene which so remarkably characterises Mr Wills's "Charles I." As thus published, the action takes place in nine different localities,—one less than in "Harold."   In presenting the drama to the reader, I have refrained from any artificial (if I may so call it) restriction of the Scenes, such as I have shown may be advantageous for the Theatre,— except in so far as I have placed the first appearance of Robespierre (Act ii. scene 1) in a Street-scene, instead of (as in the original MS.) in his then plainly-furnished residence, as a contrast to his subsequent sumptuously-furnished apartments, as shown in his second appearance in Act iii. scene 1.   But should this drama be represented on the stage, the different localities may readily be reduced from nine to seven; by condensing the Street-scenes in Paris (at present two, and hardly different) into one ; and also by making the interview between Robespierre and Collot, at the opening of the Third Act, take place in the same locality, which can be done by making Collot allude to the busts, &c., in Robespierre's house, instead of pointing to them.

R. H. P.

LONDON, *January* 1877.

ROBESPIERRE

ROBESPIERRE.

ACT I.

SCENE I.—*Place in Paris, adjoining the Gardens of the Tuileries. Night—early morning of August* 5, 1789.

Enter LUCILLE *in sedan-chair, returning from a party, borne by Attendants carrying flambeaux. On the other side enter a Patrol, headed by an officer slightly intoxicated.*

Officer. Halt!

Attendants. Make way! We are servants of the Count Beauregard, conducting home his daughter.

Off. To the lamp-post with all Counts! Come, let us see what like the lady is.

> [LUCILLE'S *Attendants set down the chair and push him back.*

Ho! Seize these lackeys!

> [*The Patrol seize them and take their torches.*

A

The Mob (gathering round). Aha! down with aristocrats! They go to revels while we starve.

Off. (opening door of sedan-chair). Come forth, my lady fair! that I may pay my respects to beauty.

Enter CAMILLE.

Camille. What is this disturbance?

The Mob. A fair aristocrat! we've netted her for our sport.

Lucille (steps out of chair). My father is Count Beauregard. Stand aside, and let me go to him!

[*The Mob close round her.*

Cam. (rushing forward, pushes off the Officer, and points his sword to his breast). See here! I am an officer as well as you: and if you dare to molest the lady! . . . (*To soldiers*). I am the senior of this drunken brute. Release those men.

The Mob (threatening Camille). Who is this would spoil our sport?

Cam. Cowardly ruffians! (*To soldiers*). I place that man in arrest. Form up,—and let the bearers pass. (*To Lucille*). Lady! allow me to hand you to your chair. Let me apologise for the affront of this drunken officer. It is not thus that France makes war against the aristocrats. [*The soldiers keep off the Mob.*

Luc. I thank you, sir, for this great service. France,

too, ought to thank you for saving the name of Liberty
from disgrace.

   Cam. (*Admiring her*). Permit me, lady!

       [*Hands her into the sedan-chair. The Attendants
          resume their torches, and exeunt with* LUCILLE.

To meet her thus! my Dream! my Angel fair!

   (*Remains in front, musingly. Day begins to break.*)

O France! my France! a new day's dawning

For thee and for the world!

I see the Future lift her golden veil,

Revealing glorious days in store.

New banners are unfurled,—

Feudalism is no more.

O goodly work! The world's blessing

Waits upon France. O joy beyond expressing!

The very Morn seems conscious of new bliss,

And brightly beams upon our happiness.

       Enter ERNEST *and others.*

     (*The Place begins to fill with people.*)

  Ernest. Hast heard the news? The Nobles join the
    movement:

Nobly they've signed their privileges away.

We all are Citizens alike,

Brothers in the broad ties of human kind!

   Citizens. Long live the Nobles! Nobly have they done.

    (*The rising Sun begins to illumine the Place.*)

CHORAL SONG.

Freedom like a golden Sun is rising.
O Goddess fair,
Beyond compare!
Now let our voices with our hearts upraising
Hail the new Day!
The broadening ray
Of Freedom's sun
Will soon unite all hearts in France as one.
O joy! O peace!
Love dawns now on the world, and ne'er shall cease!

Enter COLLOT *and others.*

Collot. What foolery is this! What idle dreams!
Think you the Nobles are sincere? Not they!
Why talk in girlish strains of love and peace?
Every grand Revolution that has rendered
A nation famous, has been made, my friends,
Not with rose-water, but with blood.
With blood alone is Freedom won.
And France! she calls aloud for tyrants' blood,
To avenge not *our* wrongs only, but appease
The million manès of her oppressèd dead.

Collot's followers. Yes, blood must flow!
We'll have each tyrant's head!

    Ça ira! Ça ira!

Cam. Freedom ! not blood !   A heavenly voice is calling:
'Tis softly falling
Into our hearts from yonder dawning sky.
O lovely Seraph ! with white wings descending,
Thy pure and spotless robe extending
O'er France, our country,—make us free
From all that's base, impure, unworthy thee !
Crown this Millennium,—let all strife be o'er,
And to the world lost Paradise restore !

Enter Count Beauregard, *leaning on the arm of his*
    Nephew, *returning from the Assembly,*—Marcel.
    attending on the Count. (*The people salute them*
    respectfully).

    Cit. Long live the Nobles !   Nobly have they done !
    Col. (*aside*). What fools those bourgeois are !   Slaves
        still in heart,—
Born slaves and fools !   Faith, this will never do.
I'll to the faubourgs, and bring out the Mob.
    Raymond (*to* Count). Have we done well, in one en-
        thusiastic hour
Thus to annul our ancient privileges ?
    Count. There are grand epochs in a Nation's life
When what is old must die.   And this is one.
France groans and suffers : and to lighten her burdens,
Her chiefs, we Nobles, should be the first to give
Example of sacrifice, and nobly annul

All that bears hardly on the common throng.

Perish all privilege that doth run counter

To the grand interests of the common weal!

   Cam. (observing the COUNT).   Her Father!

       · [*Advances towards* COUNT, *and says respectfully.*

Sir, France's best thanks, and ours, attend you!

      [*The* COUNT *passes on, with the others, without*

        speaking.

   Col. and Followers (whose voices are soon drowned by those

      of CAMILLE'S *party*).

Ça ira! Blood shall flow

To make the Revolution go!

   Ern. and Cit.   No, no!   Blood must not flow

To stain our noble work with woe.

Freedom, not blood!   Our rallying-cry

Is Peace and true Fraternity!

              [*Exeunt all but* CAMILLE.

   Cam. So dies an olden world of chains and sighs.

And joy for me!   Lucille may now be mine!

Birth-rank doth now its baseless claims resign,

And noble Love may win its rightful prize.

                  [*Exit.*

Scene   II.

Servants' Room in Count Beauregard's *House, in Paris.*

Enter Annette.

Annette. Well, things are coming to a pretty pass!
My noble master is no longer a Count, only a Citizen; and
Mademoiselle a *Citoyenne,* just like poor me! And every-
body is better than his neighbours. Heigh-ho! this does
not suit me. I get more civility from the Nobles who
come here than from the very tradesmen who bring us
eggs and butter.

Enter Marcel.

Marcel (not seeing Annette). Troubles! troubles!
  both in Court and camp.
I'd rather take to arms again, and follow
My master to the field, than thus be bearded
At every turn by the mere scum of Paris.

Ann. Ah Marcel! I am glad the Count is done with
you. I want your help.

Mar. Ha, my pretty child! an old soldier is ever ready
either for fray or feast,—to face the gleaming of the
bayonet's steel or the more killing glance of beauty's
eyes,—like yours, Annette.

Ann. What pretty compliments you old soldiers pay!

So different from the young men now-a-days. There's
François, for example.   .   .   .

Mar. The lucky youth! Heigh-ho! old as I am, I
envy him your fondness for him.

Ann. Old! Not you indeed! Come, there, stand up.
Upon my word, there's more good manhood in you than
in half-a-dozen François,—young and good-looking as he
is, you know. Give me a *man*, and best of all, a soldier.
But come, you have not dined.

> [*She spreads a little table,* MARCEL *helping her.*

Enter FRANÇOIS, *in uniform of the National Guard,
with cap of Liberty.*

Ann. (bursts out laughing). Good life! François, is that
you? What have you been doing with yourself?

François (grandly). France calls upon her sons. To
arms! I answer to her call. I have enrolled me in the
National Guard. Behold me, my sweet charmer! Am
I not now a soldier to your wish? Come, give me a kiss
to handsel this gay dress.

Ann. I die of laughter! Is that your nightcap? What
a horrid thing!

Fran. The cap of Liberty!

Mar. Nightcap of Liberty,—an extinguisher of all that's
worth calling Freedom!

Fran. You obsolete relic of the old *régime!* If I were
you, I'd wear anything to hide those tell-tale locks. Ha!

youth and liberty, good looks to boot,—these are the things to make one's life worth having. Is it not so, Annette? Behold your soldier-lover!

Mar. Soldier! Methinks there are no soldiers now in France. Each private thinks himself as good as his officer. Liberty and Equality! A pretty mess 'twill make with discipline.

Fran. We're done with Nobles now. New blood's the thing. I may be a general soon, Annette—as good as a Count any day; and you, as my wife, as good as Mademoiselle Lucille.

Ann. Peace, you popinjay!

Mar. 'Tis forty years and more since as a lad I was with my master the Count at Fontenoy. A tough business it was. When that terrible English column broke our centre, sweeping away the Guards and all our best troops, what saved France *then?* It was the Royal Body-Guard—each one a Noble, with the best blood of France in his veins. The Count, then but a boy, fell, shot down in that desperate rally which saved the Guards from annihilation and France from defeat. And now the Guards themselves are in revolt, bribed by that craven Orleans, who parades himself as " Egalité!"

[*They sit down at the table.*

Ann. (*to Fran.*) For shame! You call yourself a man, a soldier, and sit down in lady's company with your nightcap on!

Fran. Oh, I beg pardon.

> [*As he rises to put off his cap, the sword gets be-
> tween his legs, and he tumbles over the chair.*
> ANNETTE *and* MARCEL *exchange looks and
> smile.*

(*Reseating himself.*) Ducks! roast ducks, I do declare!
I am so fond of them.

Ann. That pleases our new soldier better than his arms!

Fran. Ah, but not better than beauty's arms! Roast
duck is nice, delicious : but there's a living duck (*putting
his arm round* ANNETTE) that's far nicer!

Ann. Keep off! Lord! what a notion of compliments
he has. A dead duck and a living one! Ha! ha! Me a
duck! *his* duck! That is being roasted indeed!

Fran. (*eating*). Liberty! Equality! No more Nobles
now. Every man is as good as his neighbour—better,
perhaps. But come, I say, this duck is monstrous tough.
He must have been some old cock of the roost who had
got too old for his functions. A little bit of the other,
please, Citoyenne.

Ann. Nay, nay. If one man's as good as another, surely
ducks should be the same.

Fran. Oh, come, you know, its too serious for joking.
I am very hungry.

Ann. A joke! Equality is a joke when it comes to
ducks, is it?

Fran. (*drinks*). Here's to Liberty and Equality!

Mar. Damn your Equality, sir! Men are not equal, and never will be. It's only a phrase to cover insolence to one's betters.

Ann. And Liberty, methinks, with you François, is only permission to make a fool of yourself.

Fran. Ah, had you seen us at our drill to-day! Woe to all invaders of the soil of France! It is so glorious to handle arms, and "stand at ease," and all the rest of it. Come, I will show you how we do.

[FRANÇOIS *rises and takes up his musket.*

Mar. Why, man! you handle your gun as if you were some old bachelor handling a baby,—afraid to let it fall, or lest it go in pieces. There! take hold of it: it won't bite you. "Present arms!"

[*As* FRANÇOIS *does it awkwardly,* MARCEL *gives the musket a slap and it falls out of his hands.*

Call you that holding a musket! (FRANÇOIS *picks up the gun, looking ashamed*). Now then, "level bayonets!" There, your right hand at your hip-joint—so! "Prepare to receive cavalry!"

[*As* FRANÇOIS *stands feebly in position,* MAR-CEL, *taking hold of the bayonet, gives a slight push,* FRANÇOIS *loses his balance and totters backward.*

Is that the way to receive a charging horse?

Fran. (*aside*). A horse! a brute, at least! (*Aloud.*) Oh, I gave way lest you might have cut your fingers.

Ann. Come, come. It's time for your civilian duties now. Go put on your livery: you don't look such a fool in it as in *that*. There will be such a meeting of the old Nobility here to-night. Come, clear away the table. I must away to wait upon my young mistress. (*Aside, and coming to front of stage.*) Ah me! with the first nobles of France at her feet, Mademoiselle Lucille turns from them all, and gives her heart to a nameless youth who one night chanced to save her from the Mob. What mischief will come of this! And to-night, during the banquet, she is to give him an interview in the garden. Oh love, love, love!   [*Exit.*

Count (from behind the scenes). Marcel! Marcel!

The COUNT *enters.*

Count (to FRANÇOIS). What means this masquerading? Take off that dress, and attend to your duties. (*To* MAR-CEL). I want you, Marcel: follow me to my room.

[*Exeunt* COUNT *and* MARCEL.

Fran. There's Liberty and Equality for you! A Royalist banquet to-night! I'll give a hint in the proper quarter: and then we'll see how these mighty courtiers like a visit of King Mob!   .

[*Exit.*

Scene III.

Street and Garden in front of Count Beauregard's *House,
with the Tuileries in the background.   Moonlight.*

Lucille *and* Annette *enter the Garden from the House.*

Luc. How sweetly yonder moon is shining!
    Dear lovely moon!
How well thy tender light suits my fond pining
    For Love's dear boon,—
Love, whose sweet silvery cords my heart's entwining,
    Like moonlight's beams,—
My young life with its magic all enshrining
    In tender dreams.
Shine sweetly, moon! dear lady moon! above,
And grant thy blessings on a maiden's love!

Ann. The noblest blood of France is here to-night,—
The gay and handsome, men of high descent,
Of courtliest bearing, and of sparkling wit.
Your Cousin Raymond, too—you can't but see
That the young gallant is in love with you.
And yet you slight them all for a nameless youth
Who one night chanced to save you from the Mob!

Luc. (*with emotion*). Oh, why am I a maiden nobly born?
Why is my young heart thus fiercely torn

'Twixt Love and Honour's call?
Yet ah! what honour can there be
In proving false, Camille, to thee?
Nature alone can make the die
That stamps Man with Nobility!

Ann. Oh, pause—reflect! On what a brink you stand!
Keep back your heart,—you ne'er can give your hand.

Luc. Have I not seen him in bold manhood's pride?
Have I not heard him pleading at my side?
Handsome and brave,—and, O Annette, a soul
Through which the sympathies of a world roll,—
To make Man blest by freedom, knowledge, love,
Earth a fair copy of the Heaven above!   .   .
Oh, would this goodly end were near!

Ann. 'Tis all a dream, I fear.

Luc. Oh, how I tremble at this secret meeting!
Yet with what yearning love my heart is beating!

　　　　　　　[*Distant sounds of the Marseillaise.*
Hark! what fierce sounds are those?

Ann.　　　　　　　The *Marseillaise,*—
The terrible new song the Mob have got.
The Prussians come, and Paris is in arms.

Luc. Thank heaven! it dies away.

Ann. And yonder comes your love.   Lo, see!   .   .   .
And now I go to guard your privacy.

　　　　　　　　　　　[*Exit.*

CAMILLE *enters from background.*

Cam. Lucille!

Luc.   Camille!

Cam. My angel!   Thanks, oh thanks for this sweet
  meeting!

I've hurried from the camp.   Ah there, e'en there,

Amid the shroud

Of sulphurous clouds

That hang o'er ended battle,

While dropping shots still rattle,—

And ah! by night,

On military vigils, your fair form was aye

Before my eyes, as in my heart your love!

Luc. Camille! oh, dear Camille!

What terrors fill my heart!

The world seems rocking underneath our feet:

A Night seems slowly settling down on France.

Cam. A brighter Day, my sweet! for France and us.

Your noble father soon will list my suit.

Luc. Never, Camille! you know not half his pride:

Yield all his titles, but ah, never me!

                    [*Music heard within.*—" *O Richard !*
                        O mon Roi !"

He banquets with our Royalist friends.

Cam.   I dread

Lest that known air by other ears be heard.

The Mob is out to-night : some mischief's brewing.
But ah! my sweet! the rapturous moments fly :
Bid me to love you, ever till I die!

 Luc. Oh, is it right for me to meet you thus?

 Cam. I look on Heaven's face, then gaze on thine,
And see there naught, dear heart! but what's divine.
Oh, let me be but as the stars above, ·
That now gaze down on thy sweet face in love!

 Luc. Camille! oh, say you love me! ere we part,—
Ere the wars tear you from my side,—my heart!

   [*Takes a chain from her neck, and places it round*
    CAMILLE'S.

There! take this chain—my mother's amulet,—
To shield your life, and make you ne'er forget.

 Cam. Lucille! Lucille! by all the stars above me,
Oh, with what yearning tenderness I love thee!
Pure as the moonlight on thy virgin face!
No force this chain shall from my neck displace.
Light of my heart! what sorrow thus to part!

 Luc. Camille! Camille! my hero and my pride!
How sweet it is to have thee by my side!
I love thee ever!
Oh, thus to sever!

      [*Distant sounds of the Mob.*

 Cam. Grim Terror lurks beneath that smiling sky.
O Heaven! and all ye stars! my earnest sigh
For thee to live,—or, ah, with thee to die!

Enter ANNETTE *hurriedly.*

Ann. Oh fly!   The Count comes suddenly!

Enter the COUNT, RAYMOND, *and others.*

(CAMILLE, *who was going, turns back.*   LUCILLE
places herself before him.)

Count. My daughter, we have missed you.   Our friends
   come
To take their leave.

Ray.   My cousin fair! good night!
How much you grudge us your sweet company!

Count (*seeing* CAM.) Ha! who is this?

Luc. (*faltering*). Father! it is a friend!

Count (*to* CAM.)   Sir, who are you?

Cam. Soldier of France and Freedom!—'tis my name.
No Noble I, yet noble all the same.

Count. Ha! a Republican that badge betrays.

                  [*Advances toward* CAMILLE.

And what is this?   My daughter's chain! .
Ah me! what pain!
Lucille! Lucille!   Oh shame! and woe to me!—
My child intriguing with an enemy!
(*Fiercely.*) Villain! how comes this here?

           [*Takes hold of the chain on* CAMILLE'S *neck.*

Cam. Let go your hold, sir!   The chain is mine:
I part not with it, save with life.

                B

Count. Ho there!   The Swiss!

> [*Some Swiss guards rush in.*
>
> Seize this intruder!

Cam. Hirelings! stand off!   Vile mercenary swords!
How long shall France endure you on her soil!

> [*Draws his sword.*

Stand off, I say!   [LUCILLE *rushes forward to interpose.*

Alarm without.   Enter Servants.

Servants. The Mob is in the house!

> [*Fierce shouts and ribald laughter.   Ça ira.*

Enter COLLOT *and* MOB.

Col. Foes to the State! traitors to France!
We heard your Royalist songs, and we are here.
Seize the Aristocrats!

> [*Sees* LUCILLE, *and is struck with her beauty.*

(*Aside.*) Ha! what a charming bird of Treason's brood!

> [*The Mob rush to seize the* COUNT.—COLLOT
> *goes towards* LUCILLE.   CAMILLE, *with* RAY-
> MOND, *places himself before the* COUNT *and*
> LUCILLE, *and appeals to the Mob.*

Cam. Know you me not?—the soldier-friend of freedom!
See this fresh scar,—on Valmy's height 'twas won.
(*Pointing to* LUCILLE.) This lady is my betrothed!

> [*The* COUNT *and* RAYMOND *start indignantly,*
> *but* LUCILLE *holds up her hand beseeching*
> *silence.*

(*Pointing to* COUNT.) And he the Noble who first gave his
    vote

On that grand night when Feudalism died,

  The Mob. Yes, yes! we know Camille—France's young
    sword!

And Robespierre's friend! (LUCILLE *shudders.*) Yes, yes!
    let's go:

The morning breaks, and higher work to do.

Our brethren wait us.   Arm, and to the Palace!

The Tuileries! to the Tuileries!   [*The Mob withdraw.*

> [*Exeunt* COUNT *and party into House.* LUCILLE
> *turning and looking back at* CAMILLE.

  Col. (*to* CAM.) Ha! you have baffled me.   Beware my
    wrath.

Soon shall you see whose power is greatest, friend!

[Exit CAMILLE.

(*Looking after* LUCILLE.) What a sweet dainty piece of
    love she is!

I'll mark her down, like quarry, for my prize.

[Exit.

SCENE IV.—*Same Place.*

Music from Orchestra as the Night gives place to Morning.

Enter RAYMOND *from House, buckling on his sword.*

Ray. A troubled Night is past : but newborn Day ·
Its mother's likeness wears in uglier guise.
The City moans as with a gathering storm.
By Mars ! these fierce surprises stir my blood,—
A startling change, i' faith, from courtly ease.
Come then, my sword ! be ready to my hand.

[Picks up a glove.

A lady's glove ! Lucille's ! Yes, here she stood
Last night in parley with that upstart stranger.
What meant it all ? She cannot be in love
With this Camille—Republican, *roturier*. . . .
Yet why this painful flutter at my heart ?
I love Lucille—yes, truly ; but is it more
Than cousinly affection ? This new warmth,—
Surely it springs but from this troubled hour,—
Devotion such as bounteous Nature stirs
In common Manhood from the ties of blood,—
Born of the perils which, with mushroom growth,
Her young life now o'ershadow. My sweet playmate !
'Sdeath ! I can't bear the thought : it cannot be
She loves another !   . Ah ! how this strange surprise

Doth lift the curtain from my heart, and show
That 'neath the mantle of familiar kindness,
Has lurked unseen the regal passion, Love!

> [*Looks out and listens. Shouts of Mob in the*
> *distance.*

Has Paris gone mad? With hostile armies camped
Upon our soil—ay, almost at the gates,
We fight among ourselves! The tocsin sounds,
And some new bloody work's in hand.

Enter COUNT, LUCILLE, *and* NOBLES *from the House.*

Count. My child! it threatens to be a woful day.
Keep close within the house: venture not out.
For me, my place is with our menaced King.

Luc. Ah me! how can I rest! The King in danger;
And you too, my loved father!

Count.　　　　　　　　　　Leave us now:
Observe my warning,—keep you in the house.

> [*Exit* LUCILLE.

(*To the Nobles.*) To the Palace, my friends! Our place is
　　with the King!

Nobles. To the Palace! to the Palace!
The King to save!

Count.　　　　　Ah! can aught save?
The Army wavers: there's no chief to lead,—
No iron hand to save France in her need.
The Mob is out, in hellish rout;

And nerveless hands let fall the reins of power.
O woful hour!

NOBLES (*in Chorus*).
"*O Richard! O mon Roi!*
L'univers t'abandonne.
Sur la terre il n'est donc que moi
Qui s'intéresse à ta personne!"

Count. To the Palace!   [*Sound of drums, &c.*
Hark the hoarse voices of the gathering storm!

[*Exeunt.*

Enter FRANÇOIS, *from the House.*

Fran. Annette won't have me: and coquettes with
Marcel! I am refused for my devotion to Liberty and
France,—refused, too, for a greybeard who says he was
once a soldier, and who thinks that Counts are better
than other men. 'Sdeath! I'll not stand it!

[*Other Servants come out in the uniform of the
National Guard.*

Servants. Come, François! come! Where is your uniform? There is to be a regular fight to-day. Hurrah for
Liberty! Come on!   [*Exeunt.*

Fran. A regular fight! ahem! I don't know about that.
I don't get pay, and wherefore should I fight? A man is
not bound to serve who does not get regular wages.
[*Sound of cannon.*] A regular fight, sure enough! I don't
like those big guns. I think I'll go back again. (*Goes*

towards the door of the house.)   But when France calls me
—when the Prussians come—that will be a different affair.
Then shall I charge at the head of my company—for I
am sure to be made an officer before then—and turn the
tide of battle to the cry of "Victory or Death!"   No, not
Death exactly!

[*Fumbles in his pockets for key of the door.*

Enter COLLOT.

Col. Why, that is the servant of the Count, who has
entered my regiment, and informed about his master's
banquet with the Nobles,—which I flatter myself I spoiled
for them.   (*To* FRANÇOIS.) Hollo, citizen François! why
not in uniform, and with your regiment?

Fran. (*recognising* COLLOT).   My uniform?   Yes, I am
going for it.

Col. Going for it?

Fran. Yes, I've nearly got it now.   My master, the
Count—I mean Citizen Beauregard—is not of our way of
thinking, you know; and my only chance of obeying my
country's call was to wait till he was gone.

Col. The Count is out, then?

Fran. Gone to the Tuileries, with a lot of other Nobles
—Citizens, I mean.

Col. (*aside*).   Ha! here is a chance of seeing my young
bird of Treason!   (*To* FRAN.) Hark ye, young man!
don't try to impose upon me.   You are a coward!

Fran. A coward! How dare you say so to a son of France?

Col. My friend, I don't know who your mother was: but you're a coward! Come, don't make a fuss. I see it clearly. And, as your captain, I could have you hanged for your poltroonery. A word from me would be enough. But look ye, to-day I will find you pleasanter work than facing cannon and bayonets. You may stay at home,— provided you prove faithful.

Fran. Captain, yours devotedly! A soldier of France knows how to obey his officer—(*aside*) especially when told to stay at home!

[MARCEL *appears at a window above, looking out.*

Col. The *Citoyenne* is within?

Fran. Yes, Captain.

Col. Well, stay you at home to protect her, and look after the house. But, hark ye! leave yonder gate as it is, unbarred. Do you see?

Fran. Yes, Captain. (*Aside.*) I wonder what the ugly brute is after?

Col. And should I come on duty, fail not to admit your officer.

Fran. (*hesitatingly*). Yes, Captain.

Col. Remember! Or, as sure as we'll dethrone the King to-day, I'll have you hanged, for the double crime of cowardice and of treason.   [*Exit.*

Fran. Hanged! Humph!   [*Exit into House.*

Mar. (*at window*). There's mischief brewing. Now,
shall I break this young puppy's neck—or what?

                    [*Withdraws into House.*

    (*Sound of cannon. Sacking of the Tuileries in* ˋ
            background.)

      Enter CAMILLE *and* ERNEST, *in front.*

  Ern. Oh, shame for France! Oh, shame!
Were I the King, or General of his,
I'd sweep that Mob with grapeshot from the streets!
'Twill come to that at last. It *must,*—
Or Order, Law, and Civilisation perish,
And France fall back into a night of savagery.
I told you what your dreams would come to:
Behold them realised!

  Cam. Nay, nay!—a brutal passing orgy of the Mob!
The King's a traitor,—holding with the Allies,
Whose grasp is now upon the throat of France.
'Tis right to dethrone him! Justice be done!

      (*The Mob now come to the front.*)

  1*st Citizen.* Now Liberty is gained!

    Hurrah!

With traitors' blood the Palace-steps are stained.

    Ça ira! ça ira!

  2*d Cit.* The People reigns!

Away with Kings! they tremble on their thrones,
Yet gloat to listen their crushed people's groans.

3*d Cit.* France shall set free the world.

The Tricolor unfurled,

Our banners shall make circuit of the world.

From Paris to Moscow

We'll rid the world of woe.

War to the Palace !—to the cottage peace !

While a King reigns, grim war will never cease.

4*th Cit.* Blood ! blood ! blood !

'Tis Liberty's dainty food !

Cam. Freedom ! not blood !   Let no man die !

Remember true Fraternity !

Our watchword is Humanity !

Ern. Freedom and Peace, since earth began,

And Love, are the best Rights of Man !

Col. (pointing derisively to CAM. *and* ERN.) Hark to
   those young drivelling fools,—

For any royal traitor ready tools !

Cam. (half drawing his sword). Insult a soldier of
   France and Freedom !   .   .   .

Col. Tush !   I have better work than fight with you.

(*To Mob.*) Death to the *rich!* my friends : *their* turn
   comes next.   [*Exit.*

The Mob. Death to the King ! to Traitors death !

1*st Cit.* Property is theft !

Fire at the coat !

Of this be sure,

The Rich feed on the Poor !

4th Cit. Blood! blood! blood!

'Tis Liberty's prime food.

    Ça ira !

Saint Guillotine is Liberty's queen!

LUCILLE *rushes in from the House, guarded by* MARCEL
and pursued by COLLOT.

Col. Seize the young traitress!

        [CAMILLE *and* ERNEST *interpose.*

A MESSENGER *rushes in.   Shouts without.*

Mes. The Prussians are at the gates!

    [CAMILLE, *entrusting* LUCILLE *to* MARCEL, *who
        hurries her away, diverts the attention of the
        Mob, by drawing his sword, and exclaiming :*

Cam. On to the foe! our country calls us!

All. On to the foe ! on to the foe !

To arms! to arms!

Cries without. WOMEN *and others rush in, affrighted.*

CHORUS (*the Marseillaise*).

" *Ye sons of France, awake to glory !*
    Harh ! hark ! what myriads bid you rise !
    Your children, wives, and grandsires hoary,
    Behold their tears and hear their cries !

Shall foreign tyrants, hither leading
  Their hireling hosts, a ruffian band,
  Affright and desolate the land,
While Peace and Liberty lie bleeding ?
To arms ! to arms ! ye brave !
The avenging sword unsheath !
March on ! march on ! all hearts resolved
On Liberty or Death !"

END OF ACT I.

ACT II.

___

SCENE I.—*Place in Paris, same as 1st Scene of Act I.*

Enter ROBESPIERRE, *holding a scroll.*

Robes. Here, then, the indictment 'gainst the traitor
    Capet!
No peace for France while he remains alive.
(*After a pause.*) And what are Kings, to a great People free
And worthy of Man's birthright, Liberty?
They've had their day!   Whate'er their worth
In bygone times of mankind's infancy,
Kings are now gilded pageants, void of use,
Fattening in sloth and pleasure on our fruits;
While honest myriads toil in age and want,
Scrambling, as beggars, for a crust of bread.

Enter COLLOT, *agitated.*

Col. The Army is in revolt!   Dumourier vows
He'll march on Paris, and release the King!

Robes. All treason fails against our great Republic!

Col. They say he'll soon be here. Think you 'twere well
To kill the King at once, before aid comes?

> [*Scanning* ROBESPIERRE *narrowly, and speaking hesitatingly.*

Or is it better . . . to make terms?

Robes.   Poor coward!
Have you no faith in Liberty's great cause?
We'll seize Dumourier even in his camp.
Camille has gone, with the Assembly's decree,
To recall the soldiers to their loyalty.

Col. (*aside*). There is more power in bayonets than in
> paper.

I'll keep aloof, until I see which way
The wind doth blow, and trim my sails to catch it.
(*To Robes.*) I go to call the citizens to arms!   [*Exit.*

Robes. Perish the King! The People must be free!
Perish the Nobles, and Feudality!
Perish the Priests, who cover Earth's fair face
With hideous terrors of a Superstition
Devised to keep mankind in slavery,
To bolster up an effete Society.
My faith is in the pure and virtuous People,
Simple and justice-loving. All must fall
To give free scope to the great Rights of Man,—
Instinct divine of the pure People's heart:
The voice of the People is the voice of God!

(*After a short pause.*) Traitor Dumourier! France calls
    you to her bar!
The crisis terrible,—but we shall prevail.
My hope is in Camille.   That gallant youth
Succeeds in all, and goes straight to his aim
Like falcon swooping swiftly on its game.
Just as he stopped the Royal Flight, so will
Fortune befriend him in this peril still.

Enter CAMILLE.

    Cam. The Assembly triumphs!   The Army has proved
    true!
Dumourier, baffled, now has ta'en to flight,
˙And seeks a refuge in the German camp.
    Robes. Thanks, thanks, young soldier—France's bravest
    sword!
    Cam. A Deputation from the Army comes
To vow its loyalty at the Assembly's bar.
I hastened in advance to bring the news.
    Robes. And welcome news it is—thrice happy news
For France and Liberty!   Now then, full sure,
We have the traitor Bourbon in our power!
                        [*Walks up and down.*
    Cam. Sir, I must speak—to plead for clemency!
For the now helpless Bourbons let me speak.
Ah! had you seen the Captives—piteous sight!—
Stopped in their flight, like birds escaping free

From toiler's net, redoomed to captivity :
The King most grieving for his wife and children ;
And the fair Queen, her gaiety all gone,
Mourning in tears for husband and her babes :—
A sad and stately sorrow,—not a word
Or murmur against France; but sadly all
Resigning them to ignominious bonds,
And to a future pregnant with grim terrors !
Amid my joy for France, that deep distress
Made me remorseful for my own success.

   Robes. (*who has shown signs of impatience and anger*).
Camille, I pardon you.   You're young—a soldier.
Living in camps, the only foe you see
Or know is the embattled enemy,—
The foemen from without, the ranks who wear
The hated uniforms of Germany.
You think not of the foes within—worst foes of all—
King, nobles, priests, friends of the old *régime*,—
Ay, and of foes who mix with us as friends,
Who echo Freedom's praise in the Assembly,
Yet fain would see our glorious work undone,—
Men like the Girondists, who have put their hand
To the plough at starting, yet would now turn back;
Like the accursèd brood of Lot, who, fleeing, turned
And wept for the doomed Cities of the Plain.
Such men abound : they watch for every chance
To libel the fair fame of the Republic,

And get them back into the old *régime*.
The King's their corner-stone.   While he remains,
France halts in doubt, oblivious of past chains,
And Liberty may lose the fruit of all our pains.

   Cam. I am a soldier, and would fight to death
Against proud Germany and all foreign foes.
But the Army murmurs thus to shed our blood
Only to keep in power the lawless Mob—
The ruthless, brutal Mob.   I never come
To Paris, but I sicken at the sights
And cries throughout the night, "*A la lanterne !*"
Oh, chain that Mob, and use thy power to heal
The wounds of France !   Let not foul Riot be
Crowned in the fair name and guise of Liberty !

   Robes. Young man ! what dost thou take me for ?   Am I
Some monster hardened 'gainst humanity ?
Think'st me more dull than thou to Mercy's call ?
Less ardent, tender for the good of all ?
Glows my heart less than thine with generous flame ?
Dost thou forget how France first heard my name ?
It was in protest 'gainst State cruelty,—
It was by pleading that no man should die
For ought offending 'gainst Society,—
That Life is sacred, a most sacred thing,
Inviolate alike by Law or King,—
That no mere being who as mortal lives
Has right to quench the life that Nature gives ?

C

I hold the same creed still.
But these times are exceptional.   Old things must die
To clear the way for new vitality.
'Tis Nature's law.   All Progress works by Death.
To build anew, we must erase the old. -
Better some men should die, and not a Nation.
What does a shepherd, watching o'er his flock,
But first destroy the wolves that haunt his fields,
That so the flock may live and thrive in peace?   .
A passing crisis this,—*after*, no death!

    Cam. It may be so.   Thank God, no statesman I,
To have to deal with such calamity.
But spare the herd at least.   And there is one
For whom I claim your clemency.
If I have done good service unto France,
Let Beauregard, ta'en captive with the King,
Go free,—he only acted in pure loyalty.

    Robes. He aided the escape!—a deed which might
Have placed the Invaders' heel on France's neck.
Those Nobles all are traitors,—and they must
Be swept away, ere Liberty can reign.
France owes you much: I take note of your suit:
Meanwhile the life of Beauregard is spared.

    Cam. Now France is safe, let clemency prevail;
With peace and mercy our good fortune hail!
Oh, let me have the joy
To have saved France, yet not the King destroy!

Ah, now *for all* let clemency prevail!

Robes. Yes, yes, young man! I promise you it shall,
When the last foes are conquered to my will.
And you shall see a happy France again,
Nay, for first time—a halcyon age for man,—
A peace ne'er dreamt of since the world began,—
France a new Eden. And a world's cries
Of joy will usher in new Paradise!   [*Exeunt.*

SCENE II.

Ante-chamber of COUNT BEAUREGARD'S *House, in Paris.*

Enter LUCILLE.

Luc. O weary hours and days! The sunshine's gone,
The joyous light that round my young life played!
A helpless prisoner in this lonely house,
Scarce safe by Camille's influence from the Mob
And from the intrusion of that hideous Collot.
Not daring to cross the threshold, which Marcel guards;
And each day trembling for my father, prisoned still
For his true loyalty. Father! my dear father!
The loving guardian of my motherless youth,
Oh, how I yearn to see thee once again,
To clasp my longing arms around thy neck,

And lay my head upon that manly breast
Where ever thy child's heart has found a home!
(*After a pause.*) Camille still writes to give me hope.
O good Camille! how loyal is thy love!
Would that thou wert a Royalist, like my father.
Or like my cousin Raymond, now an exile
From France for fighting for his King.   O Camille!
Wert thou but Raymond, easy would it be
For love to make its choice—as I have done!

Enter MARCEL.

Mar. Two strangers at the gate.   One begs admittance
To see my lady.   Both are poor in dress,
But one seems master and the other servant.

Luc. Do not admit them, Marcel.   Who can tell
What purpose brings them hither?

· *Mar.* They are but two : the household all is faithful.
Old as I am, I'd fear them not myself.

Luc. No, no! they must not enter.

Enter SERVANT.

Ser. (*to Marcel*).   The stranger sends this ring, as a token,
to our mistress.

[MARCEL *hands the ring to* LUCILLE.

Luc. 'Tis from my cousin Raymond! what can this
mean?

It cannot be himself.   He could not venture—

He, a proscribed man—to be here in Paris.

Well, let the stranger enter.   But remain,

My trusty Marcel, till you see all safe.   [*Exit* Marcel.

Enter Raymond *and attendant, with* Marcel. Ray-
    mond *throws off his disguise and gives it to attendant,*
    who withdraws.

Ray. Fair cousin ! dear Lucille !

Luc. Raymond ! dear Raymond ! But how came you
       hither ?

Ray. I heard the Count's in prison—doomed to death.

I could not rest away beyond the Rhine.

I longed to know your fate.   I feared each day

To hear of the Count's death : and oh ! I trembled

To think of all that might befall his child,—

My cousin, the loved playmate of my youth.

   Luc. My brave good Raymond !   'Tis a welcome
     pleasure

To see beside me a dear friend again.   [*Exit* Marcel.

I live in terror here.   Oh, I am so helpless,

And so forlorn !

   Ray. I have a passport for you.   Fly with me !

Escape the horrors of this turbulent city,

Where men become demons in their thirst for blood.

Fly with me and be safe.   O dear Lucille !

My cousin and old playmate, hearken to me !

I've come—proscribed man as I am—through all
The hosts of France, disguised, and brave the perils
Of this fierce maddened city, that I might
See you once more and offer you my love,
And beg you to be mine, and make you safe.
Here now I stand, in city full of foes,
And ask you to be mine, and fly with me.

   Luc. It cannot be. I will not leave my father.

   Ray. Cousin! not this a time for sweet smooth
     speeches.

Fain would I strengthen thee in thy dear hopes:
But when, beneath this monstrous Reign of Terror,
Have e'er the prison-doors unbarred to let
A Royalist, still less a Royalist Count, go free?
Pardon, Lucille! My heart bleeds at the words
My tongue must utter. But never, my poor child!
Will e'er the prison let go its noble captive
Save for that goal which waits all Virtue now—
The scaffold!

   Luc. Oh, say not so! My father doomed!
The thought kills *me!* But, Raymond, there is hope—
Yes, there is hope for me, and him, my father!
I have . . there is a friend, who influence has
With Robespierre . . .

   Ray.   With Robespierre!

   Luc. And he—that friend—gives us good hope that soon
My father will be free.

Ray. A friend of Robespierre! Oh, 'tis all a snare!
Lucille, Lucille! on what a gulf you stand!
Have you not heard what wiles those monsters use—
Of daughters lured to shame, by solemn pledge
Of mercy to the father, never kept?
A friend of Robespierre's calls himself your friend,
And you—what madness! Say, who is this "friend"?

   Luc. Oh, ask me not!

   Ray.   What mystery is this?

   Luc. Let me believe! My life—nay, all that makes
My life worth having, hangs on that belief.

   Ray. O cruel fate, to make me speak the words!
Lucille, I see thee orphaned: and what then?
What hope for thee, thou dear and lovely creature,
Amid the brutal licence of the times?
No prospect save one which thy pure noble soul
Would shrink from as far worse than many deaths.
Believe not their smooth words,—'tis all a snare
Fly with me, dear one! ere it be too late.

   Luc. I cannot, will not go! My flight,
It would but jeopardise my father more.
No! while he lives, I will not move from hence.
It is my answer! Go alone, kind Raymond!
Brave loyal heart! go save yourself. For me,
Here will I wait, and brave whate'er befall.

   Ray. My heart is overwhelmed in its despair!
Hear me, Lucille! I cannot leave you thus.

There is but one hope for you : and my life
Is a poor jewel to barter for your safety.
I, too—I will not go.   Come what may—
And 'tis at worst but Death—I'll gain admittance,
Disguised, to your father's cell.   They are not strict
To ope the gates for those who enter in,—
Their only care that entrants ne'er go out.
I'll dress the noble Count in my disguises :
He shall return to you,—and I remain,
And meet death happy, knowing you are safe.
Say, then, farewell to me.   A last farewell !

   Luc. Raymond ! Raymond ! brave, kind heart and true !
How can I send you thus to certain death ?
My father ! oh, my father ! . . . My brain reels
Beneath the terrors of this woful hour !

              [*Throws herself into a chair, sobbing.*

   Ray. Nay, 'tis a poor gift I offer you,—a life
Worthless without thee—a life whose sole worth now
Is that I may give it in purchase of your safety.

           Enter MARCEL.

   Mar. Here is a letter, lady.

   Luc. 'Tis from Camille ! What tidings does he send ?
(*Reads.*) " At last I have succeeded. I have obtained
" an order for the Count's release,—provided that he quit
" Paris, and live in seclusion in his country-seat at Nantes.
" To-morrow he will be free."

O happy news ! Read that letter, Raymond.

To-morrow ! oh, thank Heaven ! Joy at last !

To-morrow my loved father will be here !

   Ray. Yes, happy tidings ! Double joy ! Your father

      now

Himself will grant his sanction to my suit.

When we were children playing by the shore

Of the bright Loire, how often did he say—

He, the widowed guardian of his darling child—

That one day we should wed ! Yes, I will wait

For the glad morrow ; and then fly with you.

      RAYMOND'S *Servant enters.*

   Ser. Pardon, my lord ! but in half an hour

The city gates will close. We must begone.   [*Exit.*

   Ray. Never ! Though Robespierre's spies be on my

      track,

I'll stay, whate'er befall.

   Luc. Go, Raymond ! go ! My father now is safe :

And I, too, safe with him. Risk not your life

By madly staying when your task is done.

   Ray. Done ! I came hither through a hundred perils,

To bring you aid and save you, dear Lucille !

To bear you, orphaned as I deemed you, far from hence.

And now you bid me go ! Your father—for whose life

I was ready to give mine to certain death—

Is safe, or seems so : and now you bid me go,

Like some uncared-for slave whose work is done!
O my Lucille! though for first time my tongue
Declares my love, here amid danger and in your distress,
Oft must thine eyes have seen that love shine through
Amid the courtly life of the past time.
I stand in peril now: I woo thee on the brink
Of ruin, perchance of death.   Have you no word,
No single word of love to give me?
Fly with me now: or let me stay and hear
Thy noble father's sanction to my suit.

 Luc. Raymond, you torture me!   It cannot be!

 Ray. Cannot? and wherefore?   Do you love me not?

 Luc. Raymond, what do you force me to say?
Ever since childhood we have been dear friends;
And now, nobly as any Paladin of old,
You have taken your life in your hand, to come to me,
To save me—e'en to give your life in ransom for my father;
How can I thank you? how admire, revere,
And ever bless you?   But—I love—I love another!

 Ray. Another!   Heavens! how all my heart's fond
  dreams
Are crushed!   What unexpected blow is this!
Another!   Say, who is he?

 Luc. He who has guarded this my orphaned home,
And who now saves my father,—Camille!

 Ray. Camille! the Republican! the friend of Robespierre!

The man whose sword upbears this Reign of Terror!

It cannot be!　Lucille, the loveliest flower

Of French nobility—my Lucille—her father's child,

In love with a base Republican!

　　Luc. "Base!"—never speak the word!

　　Ray. Your pardon!　I have no right to call him so—

Him whom you honour with your love.　.　.　.

For me, my dream of happy life is gone!

What reck I what comes next?

The gates are closed,—my passport's worthless now:

Nor would I, if I could, return to spend

My worthless days safe in inglorious exile.

　　Luc. (*aside*). Oh, that I could speak to him!

　　Ray. O cousin! there are troubles yet in store

For you, your father too—believe me.　Yet

You send me like a worthless dog away.　.　.　.

　　Luc. Oh, say it not!

　　Ray. And give your love—that love which was my

　　　　dream—

In a strange quarter for a Noble's daughter.

Say, does your father know?　Has he given his sanction?

　　Luc. Be not cruel!　Ask me not now!

　　Ray. Then there is hope!　Yes, I will stay in France—

Ay, *without* hope, in simple heart-devotedness.

　　Luc. No, no!　Regain your safety o'er the Rhine.

Risk not a life so gallant and so good.

Keep it for one fairer and worthier far

Than she who thanks you,—oh, so warmly, Raymond!
For your most noble service.   Ne'er will I forget
This act of thine, which adds a crowning glory
To the sweet memories of our comrade youth.
There, go!   Bless you, dear Raymond!—bless you!
Oh, do not part from me in anger!

   Ray. May Heaven bless you! . . . Objectless I go
From thy loved presence,—my only prayer
That I may serve you yet, before I die!

   Luc. What madness, Raymond!   Peril not thy life!

                   [*Exit* RAYMOND.

O noble heart and true!

               Annette!   Annette!

          Enter ANNETTE.

'Twixt joy and grief, my heart is ready to break.
Help me, Annette!   I feel so weak and pained!

       [*Falls on* ANNETTE'S *shoulder and weeps.*

   Ann. Dear lady, be comforted!   Marcel says
In a few hours your father will be here.

       [*Supports her Mistress off the stage.*

Scene III.

Place in Paris, same as in 1st Scene of Act I.

Enter Camille.

Cam. My hopes! my hopes!—they melt in air.
The lovely Dawn is lost in lurid clouds.
The fierce Mob rules,—and everywhere
Is blood, horrid blood!
Earth up to Heaven cries aloud,
Shuddering blood-drenched by slaughter of her children
Little I dreamt, three years ago,
Of all this woe.
Riot and massacre pollute our streets,
Invade each sylvan chateau's calm retreats;
And goodly lives each day are quenched in blood.
The King is dead; the Queen's fair head
Has rolled upon the scaffold. . . .
And I—am their assassin! O remorse
That e'er the gentle Fugitives I stopped!
Oh, would that hour from out my life were dropped
My hopes! Oh, like the brilliant hues of Morning
The face of wakening Earth adorning,
They shone before my eyes!
In youthful pride, all baseness scorning,

My soul with aspirations all a-glow
Was only dreaming
For France a coming Paradise
Without a foe,—
How fair the future seeming,
Vowed to the glorious trinity
Of Liberty, Equality, Fraternity !
Kind Heaven, that youthful dream restore !
My heart grows old, of its fair hopes bereft.
Is nothing left
But to deplore ?
Turn back this tide of woe.   My hopes restore,—
Make France and me exultant as before !
Yet, am I not still Robespierre's trusted arm !
My sword still aids this reign of dire alarm.
France needs my sword to check the foreign foe,—
And yet this rule steeps France herself in woe.
Oh, Heaven, direct me !   Which is Duty's call ?
Oh, let me aid the Right, whate'er befall !   (*A pause.*)
Each new day fills my heart with fresh alarm.   .   .   .

> [*Sound of drums.   The Place begins to fill with
> people.*

And hark ! behold !—that horrid sound of drums
Tells that another dismal *cortège* comes,—
The flower of France !
Heroes whose eloquence
First roused the land for Freedom !

Whose turn comes next ?   Like fabled Saturn,
The Revolution its own sons devours.

Enter COLLOT, *in official dress.*

Col. (*to Mob*). Make way, my friends ! to let the traitors
    die !
A holocaust this is to Liberty !
  Mob. Hurrah !   *Ça ira !*
Their blood must flow
To make the Revolution go !
Saint Guillotine is Liberty's queen !
    Ça ira !   Ça ira !

Enter Procession,—the GIRONDISTS *on their way to the
scaffold, guarded by soldiers.*

CHORUS.—"*Mourir pour la Patrie !*"
Girondists.—
  " *To the scaffold we march for fair Freedom !*
    We fear not the guillotine's blow.
  O France ! see our noble example :
    Arise ! your new tyrants o'erthrow !
  To die, to die for one's country,
  'Tis the death for the brave and the free !
  Oh, life is but death without Freedom !
    Fellow-countrymen, hear our appeal :

Arise! though not to avenge us,   •
      But France's torn bosom to heal.
To die, to die for our country,
'Tis the death for the brave and the free!"

[*The Procession pass es o the stage,—the chant*
      dying away.

Col. A goodly batch of traitors!
The guillotine's a friend indeed
To France and Liberty in need!
   Mob. Ça ira! Their blood must flow
To make the Revolution go!

[*Exit* COLLOT.

Women and others. Ah woe! to see the flower of
      France
To the scaffold thus advance!
Is Mercy dead? all peace departed?
France mourns her children, broken-hearted!
   Cam. Ah me! What crimes are done
Beneath the sun
In thy fair name, O Liberty!

[*Exit.*

Women and others. Sure, now the day of blood is
      o'er.
May France be happy as before!

[*Manent.*

(Fête de l'Etre Suprême.)

Enter Procession, headed by Robespierre, *as Supreme
    Pontiff, in a brilliant costume, bearing in his hands
    flowers and fruit, and attended by a band of youths,
    Choristers, in white dresses. Statues of Atheism, Dis-
    cord, and Selfishness in background.*

The People. Hail! great Apostle of Liberty!

Robes. Brothers and countrymen! the day is won!

All Freedom's foes lie low!

A new and better time's begun!

We can at length rejoice,

Lifting a Nation's voice

To hail our triumph, and the lovely Future

That opens now on France and on the world.

Behold the banners of New Faith unfurled!

> [*Takes a torch and sets fire to the Statues. As
>   they consume, an image of Wisdom appears in
>   their place.*

Atheism, Selfishness, and Discord, perish!

Crumble to dust, or vanish into air!

Quit the fair Earth you have so long enthralled!

See, in their place, bright Wisdom rise to view,

Whose blessed reign will soon make all things new.

The Church's God, how unlike that of Nature!

D

The one means Slavery, the other Freedom,—
His *fête* the joy of a great people free
In Liberty, Equality, Fraternity!
The dismal fables that so long have weighed
Upon the soul of man are now down-hurled.
The rule of Priests is dead, like that of Kings,—
Conspirators alike against Man's happiness.
Great Nature's voice is now our highest law—
A happier worship than the world e'er saw.
Away with all priestly shackles on Man's freedom!
Live and enjoy like men, without the fear
Of tyrants here, or fabled ones above.
Wisdom and Love
Aloud I now proclaim, in the great name
Of God and Liberty!

CHORAL SONG.

Choristers.—

> *O happy day! A smile spreads over Earth,*
> *And in Man's heart new joy takes birth:*
> *He's free! he's free!*
> *In heaven-born liberty.*
> *Man now is like the gods!—*
> *The fabled gods,*
> *In their abodes*
> *On high Olympus of old reigning,*
> *Serenely blest,*

No fiats false enchaining
The joys within their breast,—
Unto themselves sole law !
The sweetest vision Earth e'er saw—
Though but in dream !

> [*Exit* ROBESPIERRE, *while they sing.*

(FESTIVAL OF THE GODDESS OF REASON.)

Enter Procession, with MADAME MAILLARD *as the God-*
dess, veiled, standing in a chariot, surrounded by
ballet-dancers, as attendants. COLLOT *and others.*

Col. Ye who want idols, come and worship here—
Fair Reason ! no inanimate stock or stone,
But living form, *chef-d'œuvre* of Creation !

> [*He withdraws her veil.*

Fall, veil of Reason, before your worshippers !

Choristers.—

> *O happy season !*
> *O Goddess Reason !*
> *We bow, fair Beauty, unto thee—*
> *Emblem of felicity,*
> *And Man's true Liberty !*

Women. How beautiful their words !
Oh, beautiful ! the sweetest ever heard.

But what is it all about ?

I cannot make it out.

   Col. Now join, my friends ! in gladsome rout,—

Join in the revels !   Worship Reason !

And celebrate the glorious season !

> [*A ballet-dance, — during which the Procession,
> with the Goddess of Reason in her chariot,
> passes off the stage.*

1st Chorus.—

> *Goddess Reason ! 'tis a folly !*
> *It only means, Let us be jolly !*
> *Nature tells us what to do,—*
> *Faith ! it is right pleasant, too !*

2d Chorus.—

> *Hell's a lie, and Heaven a fable !*
> *Let's enjoy while we are able.*
> *Since Death's a sleep that knows no waking,*
> *Let's taste all joys within our taking !*

Both Choruses.—

> *Goddess Reason ! 'tis a folly !*
> *It only means, Let us be jolly !*
> *Ha ! ha ! ha ! tra-la-la !*

   Col. (*aside*). Madame Maillard in goddess' dress looks
       nice !

By the dead gods ! I'll see what is her price.

What's a plain face, with amorous heart behind?

My power at Court will make her wondrous kind.

> 1st *Cit.* (*rushing in*). Where is my wife? The minx has left me!

> 2d *Cit.* Of reason, friend! what madness has bereft thee? --

There are no wives now!

Crowd, in chorus.—

> *Goddess Reason! 'tis a folly!*
> *It only means, Let us be jolly!*
> *Ha! ha!*

A Soldier. Ay, and no husbands either!

Save for a week or so. A dozen wives.

> *Crowd.* Ha! ha!

> *Soldier.* One for each month I've had, since Freedom reigned:

A honeymoon, my friends! the whole year round.

> *Crowd.* Yes, yes! that is the thing! Let love be free!

> 1st *Cit.* Ha, there she is!—My wife! Come catch her for me.

His Wife. Be off, you fright! Since love is free,

I shall do like the rest. I'm young and pretty,

And want a lad that handsome is and witty.

(*Looking at* CAMILLE, *who enters.*) Oh, what a lovely youth!

> —a soldier too!

> [*Goes up to* CAMILLE *and sings.*

Ah, ça ira! ça ira! ça ira!
Freedom in Love is Natures greatest law.
        Ah, ça ira! ça ira! ça ira!
Let youth and beauty have their day:
Then life goes sweetly on its way! (bis.)
        Ah, ça ira! ça ira! ça ira.

                              [*Flirts with* CAMILLE.

Enter ANNETTE *disguised as a Vivandière.*

Ann. (*aside*). The wretch! Oh, if my mistress saw this!
(*To* CAMILLE.) Ha! Captain! so you flirt like all the rest.
Is there no fair one dearer to your breast?

Cam. (*looks frowningly at her; and then*)—Good heav-
    ens! that face!
Sure I have seen it,—when? and in what place?

ANNETTE (*sings*).

Since the days of Mars and Venus,
Beauty scorneth the white feather,—
Love and Arms aye go together!
Goddess Reason cannot wean us,
Nor Vulcan forge his bars between us.

My love is brave and I am charming!
To win my heart, my gallant's arming
At Glory's call.
Love and Arms go well together,
But Love in arms is best of all!

CROWD, *in chorus.*

Since the days of Mars and Venus,
Beauty loves the Soldier's feather.
Love and Arms go well together,
But Love in arms is best of all!

ANNETTE (*pretending to flirt with* CAMILLE, *gives him
a bouquet*). I bring these flowers from one whose love is
    with you,
Though she is now fast journeying far from hence.
See her handwriting!

   Cam. Lucille! 'tis from Lucille!

   Col. (*who has been eyeing them—aside*). What name was
    that?
(*To* CAMILLE.) Captain, still flirting! Who is this new
    flame?

   Cam. Pity your face won't let you do the same!

   Col. My face! my face! Before I've done with you,
We'll see, young fop! whose face will look most rue.

      [*Goes up to* ANNETTE, *and takes her round the
      waist.*
Come, pretty maid! let's see now who are you!

         [*She slaps his face, and runs off.*

   Crowd. Ha! ha!

   1st Cit.'s Wife (*to* COLLOT). You ugly! what conceit!
    No girl would have you
Were you in the whole world left the last man!

    Crowd. The last man,—ha! ha! Last man he'll never

      be!

(*To* COLLOT.) O gallows' face!

Saint Guillotine's the only maid I know

Who'd like to take you in a close embrace.

Ha! ha! ha!

> [*They jostle and jeer at* COLLOT, *who slinks off in*
> *a rage.   The Dancers now come to the front.*

CROWD, *in chorus.*

Goddess Reason! 'tis a folly!

It only means, Let us be jolly!

Ha! ha! ha!

Tra-la-la!

END OF ACT II.

ACT III.

―――

SCENE I. — *Chamber in* ROBESPIERRE'S *House.   Busts of* ROBESPIERRE, *splendid furniture, and numerous mirrors.*

COLLOT, *entering, and Servant.*

Servant. I'll tell my master, friend, that you are here.
                                           [*Exit.*
Col. (*looking around at the busts, &c.*) "Citizen" Robes-
    pierre! 'tis like a palace!
A temple of our new divinity!
Behold our Idols! (*pointing at the busts.*)
                        'Tis but a poor face
That our new god has: what an upturned nose!
Well, how a man like that should like to see
His face in marble, and his pigmy shape
In all those mirrors, beats my comprehension!
                        [*Takes up letters lying on table.*
What incense the fools offer him!   "New Messiah!"

"Son of the Supreme Being!"   Lord! what a farce!
Faith! were there a god, and he had children—
Just like myself, for instance—his son would be
A little better-looking, sure, than this! (*points to busts.*)

                                      [*Takes up another letter.*

"Regenerator of the human race!"
I wish him joy of these high-sounding titles.
What rubbish is all that fine talk of his,
As if he could put the world to rights *next week!*
Like fools, he lives for the future,—*I* for the present.
While he draws bills, I pocket ready cash,
And turn the Revolution to good profit.
A patriot should pay himself the first.   .   .   .
Ah! here he comes—this pigmy "New Messiah!"

                    Enter ROBESPIERRE.

   Col. Saviour of France!   New dangers threaten still.
As your liege spy among the Clubs, I speak.
Danton grows weary of your stern, just rule;
Hébert doth mock you as a would-be god;
And Tallien whispers, 'tis your selfish aim
To sweep all rivals from your path, and be
New King, more tyrant than the Bourbon was.
   Robes. Must I despair of France?   What do I see?
Vain all our efforts to purge France of crime.
The Executions have done nothing!   Nay,

Matters grow worse than ever.   Scoundrelism
Fills all the offices of Government,
Swarms in the Convention, rules in the Committees,—
They spoil our work by bloodshed without cause.
Profligates! hedged round by popularity,
That so the sword of Justice cannot reach them.
But come what may, I shall unmask the traitors.
The masses must be roused, the Convention purged:
Danton and Hébert, Tallien too—the whole,
Ultras and Reactionists alike,
Must be united in one grand proscription,
Or France will perish and Reaction reign.
Yes! one stroke more, and France will then be free,
And hail the reign of Truth and Liberty,
Great in the triumph of Humanity!

    Col. Your favourite, too, Camille.   .   .

    Robes. Well, evil-speaker! what of him?
No goodlier youth is there in France than he.

    Col. He loves a Noble's daughter—Lucille,
Child of that Beauregard whose life you spared—
Do you remember? at Camille's beseeching,—
That Beauregard who aided the escape
Of Capet and his family.

    Robes. It was Camille himself who stopped their flight.

    Col. True, but 'tis now to him a deep remorse.
And 'mong his comrades of the *Jeunesse Dorée*
He speaks vile things against the Reign of Terror,

By which alone you have saved France, my liege !

Robes. Ha ! I remember how he pled for clemency
For all the traitors.   Yes, let him be watched.
France grows too full of traitors of this stamp.

Col. And Beauregard, despite your clemency,
In his retreat at Nantes, excites to arms
The stupid Vendeans, and holds secret meetings
With Larochejacquelin.   'Tis time to strike !
By terror only can the Republic stand
Against the rising tide of base Reaction.

Robes. I know that treason's hatching in the West.
Come, I despatch you to the scene.   Be sure
You check their plots at once, and make all safe.
Spare not the traitors to the Human Race !

Col. I go at once : and soon the news you hear
Will rid your noble heart of this new fear.

                            [ROBESPIERRE *exit.*

Aha ! to Nantes !   At last the game goes well.
My triumph's near.   Camille ! 'tis my turn now !
And you, proud saucy Charmer ! soon I'll find
The means to tame your pride.—Lucille is mine !
(*After a pause.*) I am a libertine.   Well, let it be.
All men the same, with opportunity.
Nature smiled not upon my natal hour,
But better far than comely face is Power.
It is for power I scheme—to make amends !
The game will pay me well before it ends.

The Mob (heard shouting without).—

> Ça ira! Ça ira!
>
> Blood must flow
>
> To make the Revolution go!

Col. These are the sounds to fire the People's blood!

Aha! *Ça ira!* To Nantes I go!

There, Love and Beauty wait me as my prize,

Or else I'll see her die before my eyes!

> [*Exit.*

SCENE II.—*Before an Inn, near Nantes.*

Enter CAMILLE *and* ERNEST, *followed by* MARCEL.

Cam. Have you no post-horses?

Mar. None, sir.

Cam. Then must we wait till our tired steeds are rested.

> [*Exit* MARCEL.

My heart beats fast, as, near our journey's end,

I think of my Lucille, and ask myself

What plan have I to shield her in this crisis.

Ern. In order to save her, you must save France!

Tallien is right: we must unite—or perish.

Royalists, Girondists, Roland, Danton—all,

The Head and Heart of France, are slain in turn,

To make drear level for this Robespierre's rule,—

Grim Despot standing on a Nation's corpse.

Even the Faubourgs murmur now, and cry
" We die of famine, and he offers blood !
" Does he suppose us cannibals, to feed
" Upon the offals of the Guillotine ? "
And we are his next victims !   Needless now
To think of different views and past regrets.
The Convention's self is to be massacred
By a new rising of the Jacobin mob.
We must unite : the danger threatens all.
Down with the Tyrant ! or ourselves must fall.

   Cam. 'Tis true, my friend : and I have cast the die.
The veil at length hath fallen from my eyes.
Nothing will Robespierre satisfy
But blood, more blood.   I can no longer bear it.
And yet the choice was hard.   Hearken, Ernest :—
Last night I met with Tallien and his friends
In secret conclave in the Wood of Vincennes,
And vowed to join them,—ay, and give my life
To save our country, ere it be too late.

   Ern. It was well done.   Pity it comes so late !

   Cam. But oh, Lucille !—how can I guard her now,
Until the trying hour be past ?

Enter MARCEL, *with letter.*

Mar. This letter, just arrived, is, methinks, for you.

                                   [Exit.

Cam. 'Tis from Lucillè !   A strange fear chills my heart.

(*Reads.*) "We are in peril. Spies are round us here,

"And horrid rumours spread. My loved Camille!

"Oh, let me see thee, ere perchance we die!"

My love! oh heavens, I hasten at her call!

Yet were't not better to have stayed in Paris,

And raised at once the standard of revolt

Against the Tyrant and his merciless minions?

Too late to think of that! To Nantes at once!

In times like these, upon each moment hangs

A priceless weight of Fortune. Ho! within!

(*To* Ern.) Adieu! to Paris haste. Prepare them for the
    struggle.

In two days I return, to lend my aid,

And share your fate. It is life or death!

  Ern. Ay, life or death! We answer to the call.

France must be free, or fighting we shall fall!

      [MARCEL *enters. Exeunt with him* CAMILLE
      and ERNEST.

Enter from background COUNT RAYMOND, *disguised as
    a National Guard of Paris.*

  Ray. Here, in the old scenes again! How changed am I,

And they for me! My chateau and estates

Are now in strangers' hands; and I, their rightful lord,

Trudge wearily past them, with only a few francs—

Or rather these bits of paper, Assignats,

Issued perhaps on sale of my own property!

Well, it is wonderful upon how little
A man may live.   I, a noble of France,
With less to live on than my servants had !—
Proscribed, too—a price set on my head—
One gets accustomed even to that !

                           Ah, Lucille !

Little I reck of Fortune's cruelty
If, after all, I find thy heart and hand
Free to be mine, and willing !

                    [*Seats himself on a bench.*

Tired, and somewhat footsore with my journey.
No horse or comfortable carriage now
As once to bear me o'er those well-known roads.
Nature reminds me of my fallen state
More forcibly by tired limbs than loss of rank
And of the pageantries of courtly life.
Ho, landlord !

             Enter MARCEL.

Bring me a little wine and bread.

            [*Lays himself full length along the bench.*

    Mar. (*aside*). A National Guard.   I do not like those
       gentry.
They have a knack of leaving scores unpaid,
And coolly tell us to send in our bill
To the Government.   .   .   Why, he has fallen asleep !
Annette !

Enter Annette.

Here is another "Servant of the State,"
Who doubtless means to feed at our expense.
He makes himself at home : see, he's asleep.

       [Annette *comes forward and looks at* Raymond.

Ann. Good-looking, anyhow. [*Looks at him more closely.*

                 Marcel ! why, I've seen—

I'm sure I've seen that face before.
He looks very tired, poor fellow !   I dislike
That uniform : but sure, he is not like the rest
Of those low, brutal, cheating Republicans.
Let's give him what he wants.

     [*They bring in a loaf, and a small bottle and glass,*
        and make a noise in setting them down on the
        table. Raymond *wakes up and takes off his hat.*

Ann. (*whispers to* Mar.) How like he is to the exiled
   young Count Raymond !

     [Marcel *notices the resemblance, and he and*
     Annette *whisper together.*

Ray. (*observing them*). Can I be recognised ?   Fool that
   I was
Not to disguise myself ere I came hither !

Mar. (*to* Annette). Yes, it is he !

Ann. (*running forward, kneels, and takes his hand*). O
   sir ! you are Count Raymond !

            [Raymond *starts up.*

    E

Do not start!

Marcel and me—do you not know us, sir?

Ray. Marcel! Annette! my uncle's trusted servants!

Mar. O happy day, to see you still alive!

Ann. How anxious for your safety has my mistress been
Since that night when you came disguised to save her!

Ray. Ah me! that night! When heartless forth I went
From her dear presence, the only thought I had
Was to remain, in hope to aid her yet.
The Government still thinks me safe beyond the Rhine.
To avoid suspicion I entered the National Guard:
But now the Count is banished to his chateau,
I've hither come to see them once again,
And learn for myself. . . .

(*Abruptly.*)   Does that Camille come here?
Is he the accepted lover of Lucille?
Knows the Count of his suit?

Ann. I know not that: but well I know
Lucille doth love him—Republican though he be.

Ray. (*walking aside*).   Then my dear hopes are dead!
. . .   How oft in Paris
Have I not burned to cross this Camille's path,
And measure swords with him, and force my blood
Upon his weapon, or his blood on mine!
Ignoble thought!   I cannot give my hate
Where she gives love.   And yet, Lucille
Wed a Republican!   .   How my heart aches!

(*To* Marcel *and* Annette.) My journey's at an end!
I'll back to Paris, and join some regiment
Bound for the field.   France needs all her soldiers now
To repel the foe.   I loathe this Robespierre's rule,
But the sole boon I seek is a soldier's death.

   Mar. My lord, pray rest yourself: you're tired and worn.

   Ann. Oh no! you must not go!   There's danger enough
      still
Around the Count.   Since yesterday
They're hunting out all Royalists in this quarter.
Know you not of the *Noyades*—the frightful way
In which they drown " the suspected ". in the Loire ?

   Mar. (*looking out*). Here comes some rider post-haste—
A Republican emissary, by his scarf.
My lord, disguise yourself.

       [*Runs into house and brings out a peasant's dress.*
                Put on this dress.

   Ann. And let me shift the table to a corner,
Where you can sit unnoticed.

      Enter François, *speaking to Stable-boy.*

   Fran. There, bait my horse, and have him ready in an
      hour.
Landlord, I come on business of the State—
Important business.   See you bring me quick
Whatever's best and ready in your larder. ·

   Ann. (*aside*). 'Tis François!

Fran. (*coming face to face with them*). Marcel! Annette!
Old chip of Royalty! who would have thought
To find your head upon your shoulders yet?
And you, my old flame! Well, I'm no longer jealous:
I have espoused myself to France and Liberty!

Ann. Two wives at once! François, that's bigamy!

Mar. With two such brides, young man, I hope you
find yourself equal to your conjugal position.

Ann. What brings you here?

Fran. (*hesitatingly*). I come to order quarters for my
chief,—Robespierre's representative at Nantes—the stern
patriot, Collot.

Mar. and Ann. Collot! oh horror!

Ann. You do not mean that monster is coming here?

Fran. Indeed I do. What's worse, there's mischief
brewing for my old master, the Count Beauregard. We
are going to his chateau first.

                    [RAYMOND *starts up and listens.*
I do not like this job, but what can I do?

Mar. Do! die first!

Ann. What! give your brave old master and his
daughter to the guillotine or the *Noyades!* François!
that I should live to see you thus!

Fran. Oh, I hate it! I am sick of all this bloody work.
But what can I do? I often think of running away. I've
a good mind to do it now.   [*Sound of postilion's horn.*
    Ah, here they come!   [*Exit into house.*

Ray. (*coming forward*). Give me a horse! Let me ride on at once, and warn the Count of his danger. This is dreadful!

Mar. Not a horse left in my stable. All have been taken for the Army.

Ray. Great God! befriend us! On foot I cannot reach the chateau before these men.

Mar. I'll go with you. I know all the by-paths.

Ann. Marcel! in mercy do not leave me!

Ray. Yes, stay. Stay here, and detain them as long as you can. Break their harness, lame their horses, anything.

> [*The horn sounds again close by. Exeunt* MARCEL
> *and* ANNETTE.

This is the hour my heart has often told me of. Thank heaven, I am here! . . . But oh, too late! too late! . . If I cannot reach the chateau in time to warn and save, at least I'll perish with them!   [*Exit.*

SCENE III.

Garden of a Chateau on the Loire.   Sunset.

Enter LUCILLE.

Luc. Absent from him! Ah me! my heart is pining!
Camille! Camille!

His love with all my heart's chords is entwining:
His form before my mind's eye aye is shining.
Ah! thus apart,
The sad cry of my yearning heart is still
For thee, Camille!

Enter NURSE, *unobserved: she pretends to busy herself
with the flowers.*

O Sun! with heavenly light so calm descending
    O'er the wide plain,
To common care and toil thou bringst an ending.
    The rural swain
In his poor cabin goes to quiet sleep;
    But I—I weep;
And Night, enchantress! brings no lullaby,—
I find no rest, save in sweet dreams of thee,
Camille! Camille!
How softly flows the shining stream!
Its murmurs lull me to a dream.
I see myself again, as erst of yore,
A child wild-playing by the murmuring shore,—
'Neath those ancestral towers, which seemed to me
In my young life the whole wide world to be.
Ah me! how changed am I!
Flow on, flow on, sweet stream!
And lull me to a dream,
Camille! of thee,

Who now—who now art all the world to me!

   Nurse. O lady! rest:

Let sweet hopes fill thy breast.

Thy father, now relenting,

Will soon to thy young passion be consenting.

No more he hates your lover's name,

But listens to his deeds of fame.

Soon will those troubles all be o'er,

And France be happy as before.

   Luc. Ah me! but not in time for us—for me!

A strange foreboding of calamity

Appalleth me.

Camille! Camille! oh, come, that we may meet,

Though but in death!

Enter CAMILLE, *hurriedly.*

   Cam. My love! my own! .   Thank Heaven!

      . . . Oh, my heart! . . .

Soul of my soul! what rapture fills me!

With heavenly joy this meeting thrills me!

For life, or death!

My latest breath

Will love proclaim, and breathe thy name,

Lucille! Lucille!

   Luc..   Camille! my loved Camille!

   Cam. My heart's love! I have hastened hither,—

Danger for all! That horrid devil

Collot has got from Robespierre power
To work his will here.   .   .

Enter COUNT BEAUREGARD.

 Count (*to* CAM.) What! here again! Young soldier,
  why thus try me?
Why brave a father's anger? I owe you thanks
For warding peril, death, from us,—and chief
From my dear daughter. I own your honour,—
Your name stands linked only with noble deeds.
(*Angrily.*) But thou'rt a slave of Robespierre!—name
  accurst,
Demon raised up to welter France in blood.
Begone! begone! That fact o'erbears all else.
Begone! I say!   . . .   Life's worthless to me now,
When my own daughter loves and pleads for one
Who serves with fiends whose only passion's blood!
 Cam. Hold! hold! . .
 Count. Who have slain our King and Queen, and all
  the flower
Of France upon the scaffold,—raging wolves
Who harry homes with rapine, lust, and blood:
Ay! and who even now are at my doors!
 Cam. Robespierre's friend no more! *I am his foe!*
My blood boils fiercely 'gainst this savage rule: .
I've vowed to end it, or myself to perish!
 Luc. Camille! my brave Camille!

Count (*to* Cam.)   What sayest thou?

Cam. Freedom, not Blood! I dare the Tyrant's power:

Nor I alone : France sickens at those sights.

Last eve, ere I left Paris, we met and planned

A rising 'gainst the Tyrant. A few days more,

And we shall beard him : our cry, "Freedom or Death!"

(*After a moment's pause.*) A few days more! . . .

      O madness!

My brain reels at the thought! Collot comes here!

Collot, the brute above all other brutes. . . .

O God! O God!

    Luc. My heart's foreboding, then, is true!

    Count. Then the worst end is near!

    Luc. Camille! Camille! oh, shield me!

Let me meet death upon thy breast!

                [*Sounds of the Ça Ira.*

Father! the cruel end draws near:

Oh, death is now the least thing that I fear.

Forgive my wayward love!—forgive Camille!

                [*They kneel to the* Count.

    Count. Rise, rise! My daughter, life of my life !

Child of my heart! Young soldier, take her hand!

My blessing take! Receive her in your arms!

                [Camille *and* Lucille *embrace.*

    Count (*aside*). O Heaven! to see their love - dream

      quenched so soon :

One sole embrace for all that wealth of love!

And Death stands 'twixt them and the bridal-door.

(*To* CAMILLE *and* LUCILLE.) There! join your hands.

  I do betroth you here!—

And there is life for Love beyond the bier!

 Luc. At last, at last!

Oh, grief is past!

Camille, your bride!

 Cam. My own!

 Luc. Oh, Death has no alarms,

When I can meet it in your arms.

Oh, sweet is even Death,

Cold dismal Death,

When I can murmur with my latest breath—

Husband, Camille!

 Cam. My bride, Lucille!

   Shouts without. Enter COLLOT *and others.*

 Collot. Seize them! in the name of the law!

 His followers. Robespierre for ever! The Republic for

  ever!

Down with all traitors!

   [*They separate* LUCILLE *from* CAMILLE, *seizing*

   her and the COUNT.

 Cam. (*to Collot*). Villain! by what authority is this?

 Col. (*unfolds his commission, points to it, and says*)—I'm

  only sorry it does not include you.

Cam. O God in heaven! send help in this dire hour!

Collot. Ha! ha! my friend, your God has not the
power!

> [*The Mob shout the Ça Ira.* CAMILLE *tries to
> reach the prisoners.*

Stand off, young fool! or you shall share their doom!

> [*Exeunt all but* CAMILLE.

Cam. Paris must rise at once, or all is lost.   .   .   .

At least for me!   Oh, why do they delay?

All's ready here.

Larochejacquelin and his brave Vendeans—

Those simple-hearted and God-fearing peasants,

Who e'en when offered quarter in the battle

Refuse, and cry, "First give me back my God!"

They're ready all, to make a clean sweep here

Of Robespierre's brutal minions,

But ah! without Paris, all is vain!

Enter RAYMOND *in background, unobserved.*

Paris is the key

To ope our bars, and end this tyranny.

And countless lives, besides ours, hang on the venture.

Oh, why do Ernest and his comrades wait?

Oh, can it be my absence makes them halt?

Sure, France has still good swords and gallant hearts,

· Other than mine, to strike for Freedom's cause.

One speedy blow at Paris would save all!

I'll write to them, and bid them strike at once.   [*Writes.*

But who to bear the letter? Whom can I trust?

   Ray. (*coming forward*). Trust *me* !

   Cam. (*starting up, and drawing his sword*). Spy ! who
       are you? How came you here?

   Ray. Put up your sword ! I say, *Trust me !*

   Cam. Traitor ! your life shall pay for this intrusion.

   Ray. You are Camille, soldier of the vile Republic,

Betrothed now to Lucille de Beauregard !

   Cam. Draw, sir ! You have my secret,—and 'tis one

On which far better lives than mine depend :

But with that secret you shall not go hence.

Draw !—nor tempt me to strike you unprepared.

   Ray. Ha ! if you knew, 'tis I am tempted most !

In other time, gladly would I have met you,

Foot to foot, and sword to sword. You've robbed me

Of what my life holds dearest. You, Sir Republican !

Have won from me the love of France's fairest flower.

   Cam. Who are you ? What means all this?

   Ray. I am Count Raymond—cousin of Lucille,

Returned from exile to watch o'er her safety.

               [CAMILLE *sheathes his sword.*

You are successful. I respect her choice.

Come, take my hand. Time presses. All is lost

Unless your aid come quickly. Give me the letter.

There is no rivalry betwixt us now

Except that noblest rivalry of love,

To outdo each other in the loved one's cause.

Cam. O noble Raymond! it is you that triumph:
For you give all, yet hope for no return.

Ray. Quick, quick! the letter! I'll to Paris straight.
Your presence here avails much more than mine.

[*Takes letter.*

Enter COLLOT. RAYMOND *retires to background.*

Col. (*to* CAM.) I have a word to speak in privacy.
The Count and daughter now are in my power,—
Settled their fate within a single hour.
We are emptying our prisons into the Loire,—
A batch shall drown this eve, and they along with them:
A man of business I,—so, prithee, hear:—
You boast your love,—now prove your love sincere.
Resign the maid to me, and she shall live,—
(*Half-aside*). Though not long as a maid. . .

Cam. Wretch! dare again such brutal threats to mutter,
'Tis the last words your villanous throat shall utter!

[*Seizes* COLLOT *by the throat.*

Col. My men! my men!

[COLLOT'S *followers rush in.* CAMILLE *dashes*
COLLOT *to the ground.*

Col. Seize him! seize him!

[*They seize* CAMILLE *before he has time to draw
his sword.* RAYMOND *rushes forward and re-
leases him.*

Ray. Fly, Camille! fly!   Save yourself,
In order to save her!

Col. Down with great Robespierre's foes!
Traitors to France!   Paid spies of the Allies!

Cam. No traitor I, nor spy!   Stand off! I say.
Who comes too near shall pay for it with life.

> [*As* CAMILLE *and* RAYMOND *exeunt, fighting,*
> RAYMOND *falls stunned by a blow.*

Followers. Here's one of them at least, who's safe enough.

> [*They bring* RAYMOND *forward.*

Ray. Lucille! Lucille!   Thank God, Camille is safe!

> [*Falls, swooning.*

Col. Search the prisoner!

> [*They take the letter from his breast.*

Followers. A paper, sir.   [*Give letter to* COLLOT.

Col. Ha! here is proof at last.   Letter from Camille
To Tallien, urging him to rise 'gainst Robespierre!
A precious document indeed for me,—
A passport now to power and all life's prizes!
Power! for Power!—'tis what I've schemed for long,
And now 'tis mine!   O precious bit of paper!

Ray. (*reviving*). The letter! in his hands!

> [*Rushes upon* COLLOT, *and snatches the letter*
> *from him.*

Ha! it is safe!   Make way, ye cowardly herd!   [*Exit.*

Col. 'Sdeath! it is lost!   The traitors, too, escaped!
Follow, ye cowards!   Seize them in Robespierre's name

Dead or alive!　Come ye not back without them!

> [*His men rush off in pursuit.*

Those trusty knaves, full sure, won't let them slip.　.　.

So now!　I have the love-cup at my lip.

Vengeance upon Camille! triumph for me!

Lucille! there's now but one choice left for thee,—

'Tis Death, or me!　　　　　　　　　　[*Exit.*

SCENE IV.

The Noyades.—An Islet in the Loire.

Enter a large boat crowded with fettered prisoners. COLLOT *takes out* LUCILLE *from among the prisoners, and lands on the islet.*

Col. Now then, let go the traps!　Plunge them all in!
So die all traitors to our great Republic!

> [*The bolts are drawn, the bottom of the boat falls out, and the river is seen filled with drowning men and women.*

Col. (*to* LUCILLE). Behold the fate you have so well deserved,—
The fate for which, perchance, you are still reserved—
Your father too.　But I give you a chance,

(Like a good Providence, as you folks say!)—
Be mine! or like those drowning wretches, you
In half an hour will be, your father too.

> [*Shrieks of the drowning victims.*

Luc. Oh horror!

Col. Nay, there's no horror, save in drowning there.
Methinks we'd make a very pretty pair!

Luc. Ruffian! with demons like yourself go mate!
A Noble's daughter knows how to meet her fate!
Monster! no, never! Let me rather die. . . .

> [*Rushes to throw herself into the river.* COLLOT
> *stops her.*

Col. You are powerless in my hold.

Luc. (*struggling*). I'll rather die! . . .

Col. But then you can't, my sweet! though you should
try.

Luc. (*freeing herself from his hold*). Vile monster! yes!
a thousand deaths I'll die. . . .

Col. By hell! proud minx, but you shall live, and be
A mother of Republicans like me!
I'll make you mother of a better breed
Than ever sprang from curst Nobility.

Luc. (*falling on her knees*). Oh, help me, Heaven!
And you, O man!—if man you still can be—
Oh, let death promptly end my misery!

Col. Never! by the dead gods! You plead in
vain.

'Tis for love, only, that I give you life.

> [*Advances towards her.*

Thus shall you yield, unwed, to be my wife!

> [*They struggle.* CAMILLE *is seen swimming to
> the Islet. As* LUCILLE *falls back exhausted, he
> lands and rushes upon* COLLOT.

Cam. Monster! now meet your doom!

> [*Throws him backward into the river.*

There drown!—if any one like thou can drown,

Whose right fate is the scaffold!

> [*Raises* LUCILLE, *who slowly recovers conscious-
> ness.*

Luc. Camille! my own Camille!

> [*As the scene closes,* COLLOT *is seen floating on a
> spar in background.*

Curtain falls for a few minutes.

F

.

CONCLUDING SCENE.

The Revolutionary Tribunal. — ROBESPIERRE *and others*
seated in judgment. COLLOT, *as accuser.* CAMILLE,
COUNT BEAUREGARD, *and* LUCILLE. *Soldiers and*
Attendants.

Col. Judges! who guard the liberties of France,
And purge her soil from treason and from crime!
Behold this batch of traitors,—seized at last,
Plotting against the State and Liberty;
Abusing our great Robespierre's clemency,
Which spared them once before, when due to death.
Camille the worst of all! doubtless a spy.
And these two, relics of the old *régime*,
By my devoted service, tracked and caught,
I here denounce them in the sacred name
Of the Republic.   Judges! they must die!
Cam. No traitor I,—but foe to France's foes!
As I have fought in glorious battle oft,
And gloried in my wounds, as well as triumphs
Against the foreign foe,—oh, not less proud
Were I if, with those manacles struck off,
I could do battle 'gainst thyself, O Tyrant!
Who now doth prove my country's worst oppressor.

Behold! erect I stand,—thy wrath defy :
Ready to die
Upon the shameful scaffold, as when erst
On Valmy's heights 'gainst fearful odds I strove,
And turned the tide of battle with my blood,
Amid the shock of squadrons, cannons' roar,
Charging for France and Freedom !

    Robes. There's but one doom for them, — and that is
       Death !
Dangers now thicken round our great Republic.
France swarms with recreants, like this Camille,
Who call them friends, and yet are our worst foes.
I've done with mercy.   Blood must still faster flow.
No hope for France, till a clean sweep is made,
And naught is left but the pure virtuous People.
Collot, you're right.   In every town shall be
A man like you, to make short work of all
Who seek to thwart or murmur 'gainst our rule.
Let women sicken at the scaffold's work :
Each traitor's blood makes sweet the air of France.
Tallien and his foul brood in the Convention
Must now be seized before the sun goes down :
And these shall die with him to-morrow.
Would that our foes had but one neck, that so
France might be rescued by a single blow !

    Col. (*to Clerk*). Make out the decree at once : they die
       to-morrow !

Count (*to* COL.) Vile miscreant!   Monster in human
 form!
What mother e'er begot such hideous progeny!
 Luc. Thank heaven for death, to save me from his
 power!
(*To* CAM.) Camille! my love! no more shall Fate divide!
I shall die happy with thee at my side,
Death, although all else divide us,
Shall now at last unite us!
 Robes. (*addressing the other* JUDGES). Sign the arrest for
 Tallien and his party.
Already Henriot and his cannoneers
Summon the Convention to give up the traitors.

Enter MESSENGER.

 Mes. Henriot has failed!   His cannoneers
Refused to fire.   The Convention now proclaims
Robespierre outlawed: and calls upon the people
To rally to its aid against the Tyrant.
The *générale* is beat in every street,—
The National Guards respond to the appeal.
 Col. and others (*to* ROBES.) Proclaim yourself Dictator
 or all is lost!
Denounce the Convention as the foe of France!
 Robes. Ha! then, the crisis comes.   Let Mercy die!
I'll sweep now every foe from out my path,
Though half the Convention perish on the block.

Mes. Come, let your presence rouse the citizens,

And give fresh fire to Henriot's wavering troops.

> [*Exeunt* ROBESPIERRE *and* JUDGES. *Sound of fighting without.*

Cam. Hark to the rattle of angry battle!

Upon the street the rival forces meet,

In strife for life and liberty.

> [COLLOT *cuts the rope by which* LUCILLE *is fettered to her father; draws her away, and pointing to the other prisoners, says—*

Col. These to the scaffold at once,—and her to-morrow!

(*To* LUC.) Till then, proud minx! I'll answer for your

keeping.　　　　　　　　　[*Tries to lead her away.*

Luc. Camille! Camille! Oh, help! Oh, let me die!

Col. Come on! *This* time your lover shall not balk me.

Luc. (*struggling with* COLLOT). Camille! my father!

Help! oh, help!

> [CAMILLE *and the* COUNT *by a sudden wrench break their bonds.* CAMILLE *frees* LUCILLE *from* COLLOT *and clasps her in his arms.*

Cam. (*to* COL.) Vile wretch! stand off! At least we

die together.

Oh, for a weapon!

> [*The* COUNT *wrenches a sword from one of the soldiers and hands it to* CAMILLE.

Count. There, strike! ay, to her heart!—then give it

to me.

Luc. (baring her bosom). Here! quick, Camille! My
    love! 'tis the sole service
You now can render me.

    Cam. One moment first, to end that demon's life!

        [*Rushes at* COLLOT, *who takes refuge behind the
        soldiers.*

    Col. (to soldiers). Quick! chain those prisoners; and
    take them hence.
Should rescue threaten, shoot them on the spot!

            [*Alarms without. The soldiers hesitate.*

    Col. By the dead gods! why stand ye halting thus?

Enter ATTENDANTS *affrighted.*

    Atten. The foe prevail!—they enter at the gates!

    Col. Quick, then! let Justice do its work at once!
Fire! fire! I say. Let not these traitors escape!

        [*Some of the soldiers raise their muskets to fire.
        Shots outside.*

Enter RAYMOND *and* ERNEST, *with* MARCEL *and others,
    and place themselves between the soldiers and the
    prisoners.*

    Ray. Hold! hold! the victory's ours. The Convention
    triumphs!
Robespierre, fallen, welters in his blood.
The Tyrant falls,—the country's free;

And thankful myriads shout in ecstasy!

 Luc. Dear father! thou art safe!

        [COUNT *and* LUCILLE *embrace.*

 Ray. (to COL.) And thou, O monster of inhumanity!

      [*Seizes* COLLOT *and holds a pistol at his head.*

The murdered call for vengeance upon thee.

I only spare thee now

To let the guillotine do its work upon thee.

       [*Gives him in charge to* MARCEL.

(*Turning to* LUC.) Lucille! Thank God, my prayer has

  been heard,

And thou art saved at last.

 (*Turning to* CAM.) My rival! thou art free,—

Free for the happiness that waits for thee!

 Cam. What can I say to nobleness like this?

I yield to no man in devotedness;

But thou dost make my love look poor and pale

Seen in the light of thy grand sacrifice.

 Luc. O Raymond! noble Raymond! Soul so pure,

How can I thank thee in weak woman's words!

 Ray. Kind thoughts, from heart like thine, are as a prayer

For ever rising from the earth to Heaven,

A benison on my life. I ask not much :—

Living, a place in thy sweet memory,—

Dying, a soldier's death, in France's cause.

This Tyranny ended, I hasten to the field,

To fight the foes who would dismember France,

And crush the name of Freedom out of Europe.

> [ANNETTE *enters and throws herself into her*
> *Mistress's arms.*

Count. (*to* RAY.) Spoke like a Noble! I cannot bid
you stay.

But for my years, I'd take the field myself.

Each Frenchman's place is now in the ranks of war.

Enter FRANÇOIS.   *Goes up to* COLLOT.

Fran. You ugly monster! vulgar upstart! Who will
die first now for "the double crime of treason and
cowardice?" Ha! ha!

Ern. France now is one again,—the Tyrant falling!
From earth to heaven a voice is calling,
" Freedom! not Blood!"
Oh, may the sorrows of our country cease,
And all at length be happiness and peace!

Count (*to* CAM. *and* LUC.) Heaven smile now on you
both! and, 'midst your love,
Forget not the kind Providence above.

> [CAMILLE *and* LUCILLE *embrace.*

Luc. Sweet bloomed my youth 'mid summer skies
When the form of my hero first met my eyes.
But sorrow and terror brought night on my day,
Till for Death, as a blessing, my soul did pray.
Yet in joy or in sorrow, in hope or in fear,
Thou, ever thou, to my heart wast dear!

What joy now I feel!

Camille! Camille!

   Cam. A dream of love, oh, bright as heaven,

At sight of thee to my heart was given.

And e'en through the night of Terror and woe

That dream 'mid the darkness did brightly glow.

Now sorrow and terror and night are past,

And the dream of my heart proves true at last!

   Luc. O joy! O bliss!

   Cam. Sweet hour is this,

Which crowns my life with happiness!

CHORUS.

The Terror's o'er! and Peace descending,

Its blessing sending, true love befriending,

Crowns our life with joy unending.

Yes, France is free!   O Powers above!

Smile now on Freedom and on Love!

THE END.

WORKS BY R. H. PATTERSON.

THE NEW REVOLUTION.

Revue des Deux Mondes.

Les articles de M. Patterson, reimprimées depuis en volume sous le titre de la Nouvelle Révolution, lui aient valu la réputation de prophète, et d'ingenieux penseur politique.

The Dial.

These articles are among the ablest contributions ever made to journalism. Mr Patterson's style is clear, nervous, and dignified, and rising at times into noble though chastened eloquence. Mr Patterson would be a distinguished Historian were he not the distinguished editor of a Tory newspaper.

St James's Chronicle.

A very remarkable volume. It is a graphic and almost prophetic sketch of the policy and principles of Louis Napoleon.

Morning Advertiser.

The author is entitled to take his place in the foremost rank of the patriotic politicians of the present day.

ESSAYS IN HISTORY AND ART.

Dublin University Magazine.

Not often, whether in prose or in verse, does the same man command both "the vision and the faculty divine." Not often is the original thinker endowed with a fluent and fascinating style, which takes captive the crowd by its beauty. Mr Patterson has this good fortune. . . . By this volume Mr Patterson has shown himself as original a thinker on subjects of general History and Art as he had previously proved himself to be on the contemporary history which we call Politics. He has insight, logic, humour, a noble and variable style,—and can claim entrance by right to the first rank of authors of the day.

Athenæum.

Fine appreciative taste and original observation are found united with range of thought, and a rare command over the powers of the English language.

Revue des Deux Mondes.

C'est un plaisir assez singulier que nous a donné la lecture des *Essais* reunis de M. Patterson. . . . M. Patterson est sans doute un homme supérieur ; et il est loin de laisser faire ces instincts qui sont entrés en lui par droit de naissance—ces génies de son temperament. Quoiqu'il ait aussi son côté poétique, c'est un esprit essentiellement clair et logique,—qui aime à spéculer, et à embrasser des vastes ensembles. Dans ses instincts, comme dans son intelligence, il n'a rien d'exclusif. Une des qualités qui ont le plus contribué à sa supériorité c'est qu'il est viril. Il a le sentiment de le Realité—il ose la regarder en face : et cela n'est pas uu mince avantage.

L'Independance Belge.

C'est un de ces ouvrages qu'on ne lit pas à moitié, mais jusqu'au bout, et qu'on retrouve toujours avec plaisir.

Revue Contemporaine.

Un vif sentiment de la beauté—un langage animé, coloré, parfois lyrique—des aperçus souvent ingénieu , prêtent un charme réel à ces esquisses.

Kolnische Zeitung.

These essays are distinguished alike by profound learning and by the originality of their contents. . . . A work of genius—of eminent value.

THE ECONOMY OF CAPITAL.

Money Market Review.

A work which constitutes a full and complete exposition of our whole monetary system. But it is more than that: it is a most interesting book.

Westminster Review.

In all that really has reference to the Economy of Capital, Mr Patterson's book is most excellent. His information is complete; his style is clear, forcible, and even picturesque; and his account of the modes by which capital is economised in the banking-system, is the very best extant.

Leeds Intelligencer.

A wonderful work. A book that will in a few years be not only in every English library, but will have a world-wide reputation.

THE SCIENCE OF FINANCE.

British Quarterly Review.

'The Science of Finance' is a title which covers a wide field of thought, and Mr Patterson's book quite answers to its title He has examined elaborately and with abundant detail the questions of Currency and Banking, of Railway and Municipal Finance; and we rise from its perusal with the impression that we have rarely read a book displaying so full acquaintance with the facts relating to its subject.

London Review.

Mr Patterson, whatever he may be in politics, is a Radical in finance. He is a strong and original thinker, and his mastery of the subject is undoubted.

Morning Star.

All who are interested in the great Science of Finance cannot go to a better repository of facts and opinions than Mr Patterson has provided.

THE STATE, THE POOR, AND THE COUNTRY.

North British Daily Mail.

The ability which Mr Patterson has shown in handling some of the most difficult and pressing Economical problems, entitles him to be heard on most of the leading Social questions of the day. . . . Himself a Political Economist of mark, he finds "a heartless Political Economy (so-called, but not the true thing)" in his way. An excellent and timely volume.

Public Opinion.

The writing is clear and pointed, and truths are told with decisive firmness on a subject upon which much nonsense has been written.

Yorkshire Post.

A glowing and eloquent little book, in which, among other matters, the great problem of the *reproductive employment of pauperism* is ably stated and approximately solved.

British Quarterly Review.

A most valuable and suggestive contribution to the political literature of the day. It should be read by every one who desires to see the English a great nation—a people among whom neither tyranny nor pauperism should be possible or even conceivable.

Vanity Fair.

A very valuable contribution to the world-wide discussion that is every day growing more imminent on the momentous subject of which it treats. It is always advantageous to hear the voice of a man so thoroughly in earnest about his subject as Mr Patterson is, and who speaks so ably and in such an impartial unprejudiced way. . . . The day is fast approaching when the Nation will have to face the contemplation of a disease that saps the elements of its strength, and to devise measures for its speedy removal.

WILLIAM BLACKWOOD & SONS, Edinburgh and London.